OTHER
Harlequin Romances
by FLORA KIDD

THE TAMING OF LISA

by

FLORA KIDD

HARLEQUIN BOOKS   TORONTO
WINNIPEG

Original hard cover edition published in 1972
by Mills & Boon Limited, 17-19 Foley Street,
London W1A 1DR, England

© Flora Kidd 1972

SBN 373-01684-0

Harlequin edition published May, 1973

*All the characters in this book have no existence outside the
imagination of the Author, and have no relation whatsoever to
anyone bearing the same name or names. They are not even
distantly inspired by any individual known or unknown to the
Author, and all the incidents are pure invention.*

Printed in Canada

1684

CHAPTER I

ELISABETH ROY SMITH clutched her briefcase, a shopping bag and a bunch of chrysanthemums in one arm and fitted the key into the lock of the door of the flat where she lived. The key turned quite easily, but as usual the door did not open until she had pushed a shoulder against it. Then it opened suddenly and she almost fell into the small hallway, landing with a crash against the wall.

"Is that you, Lisa?" called a voice from the living room.

"Who else?" she called back. Who else but she would make such a rowdy, uncontrolled entrance?

Kicking the door shut with a backward flick of one shapely, booted leg, she went into the big room and deposited her load on the old-fashioned, round walnut table which was already cluttered with examples of hand-made pottery. At the table sat a small fair-haired girl of about twenty-two. She was dressed in a multi-coloured smock and was bending over a classically-shaped pottery jug on which she was painting a design, with sure quick strokes of a thick brush. She looked up, saw the dark red shaggy blooms of the chrysanthemums and her eyes widened.

"Who are those for?" she asked.

Lisa, who had been slipping off her long brown coat and tossing it carelessly over one of the armchairs, pulled off her emerald green crocheted beret, threw it on top of the coat and came across to the table. Picking up the flowers, she presented them to the fair girl with a theatrical flourish.

"For you. I thought they might cheer you up. Also I couldn't resist the colour. Aren't they gorgeous?"

"Mmmm." Mandy Atkins sniffed the shaggy blossoms and then held them at arm's length to admire them. Her gaze passed from the flowers to Lisa, who stood tall and willowy in her midi-length tweed skirt and emerald green sweater.

5

Her cunningly-cut straight dark red hair fell in a fringe over her white forehead and beneath the fringe dark eloquent eyebrows were slanted above hazel eyes which twinkled and danced, their expression indicative of the warm, lively nature of their owner.

"You're like one of them yourself," Mandy remarked impulsively. "Earthy and exotic at the same time."

Lisa raised her eyebrows in surprise and unusual colour stained her high cheekbones.

"I don't mind being considered exotic even though I'm not, but I think I draw the line at earthy," she said, glancing down the clean straight lines of her body outlined by the clinging sweater and skirt. "Do I look as if I grub in the earth for a living?"

"I didn't mean it like that," replied Mandy with a chuckle, as she began to place the flowers in a big stoneware jar. "For me earthy means rich browns, glinting greens, burning bronzes, russet reds . . . your colours."

Lisa's ever-changing eyes deepened to brown as their expression softened and she put an arm round her friend's slim shoulders and hugged her.

"Thanks for the compliment. I should have known you meant colour. Have you done much today?" she asked, waving her hand in the direction of the pottery.

Mandy sighed and grimaced.

"Not as much as I would have liked. It seems to take ages to throw off the effects of 'flu. Aren't you home early?"

Lisa twisted away restlessly and walked to the big bay window to stare out at the grey November sky.

"Yes. Hatton and I had a disagreement, so I walked out," she said in a taut voice.

Hatton's Limited was a company which designed and manufactured women's clothing. Lisa had worked there for two years ever since she had left the College of Art. The company was well-known for its original and stylish clothes and for the high quality and finish of its articles. Lisa, who had been trained in dress design, had been considered extremely lucky

6

by her friends when she had landed a job with the company, but her association with her immediate superior Richard Hatton, the chief designer, had been stormy and marked by frequent clashes of temperament, culminating in her walk out this afternoon.

"Are you going back?" asked Mandy curiously. Possessing a fairly placid temperament, she was rarely surprised by the actions of her warm-hearted, impulsive friend.

"Not even if he comes and asks me on his bended knees," replied Lisa fiercely.

The thought of the impeccable, slightly supercilious Richard Hatton on his knees in front of Lisa was too much for Mandy's sense of humour and she began to laugh.

"You can hardly expect him to do that," she said.

"Why not?" demanded Lisa, swinging round, her eyes ablaze with strongly-felt emotion. "That's where he'd like to see me. Nothing would please him more than to see me grovelling in the dust apologising, asking him to give me my job back and admitting that he was right after all."

"You didn't tell him he was wrong?" exclaimed Mandy. "That was scarcely tactful of you."

"He wasn't tactful with me, so why should I be tactful with him? He criticised one of my designs and I told him it would sell like hot cakes. So he asked me what I knew about marketing. I told him and he didn't like it. Yet if the suggestions and criticism had been made by Johnny Holmes or one of the other men he would have listened and considered them. He's like so many men. He won't accept a woman as being equal to him in intelligence and ability. He thinks women were created only to have babies, keep house, be ornamental and provide comfort for the male of the species after his hard day's work."

"Well, aren't we?" interrupted Mandy provocatively, her eyes twinkling with amusement as she realised her friend was mounted on her favourite hobbyhorse, the rights of women.

Lisa flashed her a scathing glance.

"You know very well what I mean. We're capable of much more and that should be recognised. Richard Hatton assumes that because I'm a woman I must be incapable of logical thought, which irritates me because I want to be judged by my abilities, not because of my sex."

"And to think I once believed you were in love with him!" sighed Mandy mockingly.

"I was never in love with him," asserted Lisa vehemently. "For a while I admired him for his creative ability, but . . ."

"That soon wore off and was no substitute for love," suggested Mandy, puckishly.

Lisa frowned.

"I'm not sure I know what's meant by love. I only know I couldn't love a man who has as little respect for women as Richard Hatton. Love is only possible where there's equality," she said quietly, turning to lean her forehead against the cold window pane and looking down into the dank tree-lined street of the Manchester suburb where they lived.

"How I hate November," she murmured. " 'No fruits, no flowers, no leaves, no birds, November.' Who wrote that?"

"I think it was Thomas Hood. I prefer Scott's description," replied Mandy.

" 'November's sky is chill and drear
    November's leaf is red and sear,
    All grey and crimson.' "

Then snapping out of her dreamy mood Mandy added, "I'll go and put these in water and put the kettle on. There's a letter for you from Scotland. It's on the mantelpiece."

Lisa continued to lean against the window pane, not seeing the branches of the plane trees which lined the street. The argument with Richard Hatton that afternoon had sapped a great deal of her strength and courage. It had been hard to defy him, especially when she remembered that only twelve months ago he had represented for her all she had admired and respected in a man, or so she had thought.

But she had defied him. She had stuck to her convictions and as a result she was free again. Free of his overbearing demanding ways, free to design as she wished. No longer were her emotions in thrall to his every whim. She was her own woman again, like her Great-Aunt Maud.

8

The thought of her mother's aunt reminded her of the letter and she went to the mantelpiece, took it down and stared at the fine spidery writing on the envelope. It was from Maud Roy, that formidable spinster who years ago had preferred to break off her engagement to be married rather than go through with marriage to a man for whom she had lost her respect.

Tearing the envelope open, Lisa began to read the letter. Aunt Maud had wasted no time on pleasantries but had gone straight to the point.

"I have been ill, seriously ill, and I'm not likely to get better quickly, if at all," she had written. "There is one in this village who likes to think I'm already on my last legs and that I'm ready to give in to his demand to sell my property to him. Three times I've sent him away with a flea in his ear. I've told him that when I've gone there'll be yet another Roy taking my place here at Breck House. It's the only argument that stops him, the only one he'll respect, since he's a stubborn clan-conscious Scot like myself.

"But last time he was here there was a sceptical glint in his eyes and I could tell he didn't believe me.

"This morning when I looked out of the window I saw him on the land below the shore road. He was measuring. I'm afraid he might build there and spoil my view. I could understand his attitude if he were an 'incomer' to the village, but his family has been here since the Vikings came plundering along the coast and he should know by now that we Roys hold fast to our own possessions.

"Come and see me, if you can, Elisabeth, for Christmas and the New Year holiday, so that I can show the rascal that there really is another Roy to whom I can bequeath my property. It's a long time since you were here. I'd love to see your bonny face."

Mandy came back into the room carrying the big jar of flowers. She set it on a low table and then stood back to admire the effect of the big dark red blooms against the background of pale Wedgwood blue wall. She glanced at Lisa and was surprised to see the glint of tears in her friend's eyes.

"Bad news?" she asked gently.

Lisa shook her head slowly as she pushed the letter into its envelope.

"Not really. Aunt Maud hasn't been well. She wants me to go and see her. Poor old lady, she feels she's been harassed by someone and she needs the support of another Roy."

"How long is it since you last saw her?" asked Mandy.

"Six, almost seven years. It was just before Mother and Dad left for Jamaica. Mother and I went alone." Lisa paused, swallowed and then continued in a rather desolate voice, "Sometimes I think Mother had an intuition that she wouldn't be coming back, because she insisted on taking me to Ardmont. Daddy couldn't go at the last minute because he had work to do. After Mother died I always intended to go and visit Aunt Maud again, but somehow I spent the holidays doing something else, either flying out to stay with Dad or taking trips to Europe."

"Well, there's nothing to stop you from going to see her now," remarked Mandy. "From all accounts you haven't a job, although it's my guess Richard Hatton will be on the phone this evening using all his charm to persuade you to go back. Why don't you go and have a holiday with your aunt? The change of scene might help you to unwind and to decide what you're going to do next. Kettle must be boiling."

She hurried out of the room and Lisa began to pace the floor with long swinging strides, her arms folded across her chest. Mandy's suggestion had fallen on fertile soil. Already in her imagination she was on the ferry boat crossing the wide Firth of Clyde, looking over tumbling sunlit water to the entrance of a narrow strait, or kyle as it was called in Scotland, which separated the island of Boag from the mainland. The strait led to the village of Ardmont, an old settlement dating back to the times of the Vikings, well-known as a yachting centre and seaside resort, as well as the home of what had once been a flourishing tweed industry.

Another leap of the imagination and she was in the tall grey house sitting beside Aunt Maud listening to her vigorous voice as she talked about the Roy family, of which she was the only survivor. Then she was out of the house striding across the moors at the back of the village, lingering along the shore watching the yachts swinging at the moorings or envying the crew of one as sails were hoisted and it left its mooring to sail down the kyle to the distant sea.

It would be pleasant to go for a few weeks and stay in that place of summer calm in the midst of winter. It would be good to talk to her mother's only relative, to sleep in the room beneath the eaves where her mother had slept as a girl and to walk where she had walked.

Mandy returned with the tea-tray just as the telephone rang.

"You answer," said Lisa quickly. "It might be Richard."

"What shall I say to him?" asked the unperturbed Mandy.

"Tell him I'm out. No, tell him I've gone away, far, far away, and at the moment I've no intentions of coming back," replied Lisa recklessly.

Having made the decision to go to Scotland it was not difficult to make further arrangements. A friend of Mandy's desperate for comfortable accommodation and genial companionship was only too pleased to move into the flat. A telephone call to Aunt Maud informed that lady that her great-niece would be with her soon, and in a few days Lisa stood, as she had anticipated, on the top foredeck of a ferry boat as it plunged and wallowed through four feet high waves across the wide Firth.

The weather was far wilder than Lisa had expected. There was no resemblance between this crossing of the Firth and the one she had made almost seven years previously. Today the wind tugged at the tweed cloak she was wearing, pulling it away from her body, and icy dampness penetrated her sweater and skirt. She was glad she was wearing a close-fitting knitted hat to protect her head.

Yet for all the wildness of the wind Lisa had no intention of leaving her position. She stood where she was looking over the wintry waste of water to the distant misty islands, a rather odd-looking figure in her billowing cloak and streaming,

11

brightly-coloured scarf, drawing the attention of the only other passenger who had ventured up on to the top deck.

This passenger was a small boy of about seven years of age. He was warmly dressed in long tartan pants and a navy blue duffle coat. From beneath the hood of the coat a tuft of blond hair stuck out. When he had first come up on deck he had gone up to Lisa and had stared at her for a while, but she had been so engrossed in looking out to sea that she had not noticed him. Then he had gone to play on the wooden slatted seats, walking along each of them and jumping off the ends. When he had tired of that he had disappeared down the companion-way, the steep stairs which led below. He appeared again about fifteen minutes later and sidled up to Lisa to stare at her while he sucked a lollipop someone had given to him.

This time Lisa noticed him and glancing down met the wide innocent stare of dark blue eyes set on either side of a shapely, freckled nose.

"Are you a witch?" he asked.

She smiled at him. When she smiled two dents appeared in her cheeks on either side of her mouth and her hazel eyes twinkled warmly.

"What makes you think I am?" she countered.

"You're wearing a cloak, and witches often wear cloaks, and you don't mind the wind."

"I'm not a witch. I wear a cloak because I find it warm and comfortable. I do mind the wind, but I'm not going to let it stop me from staying up here and seeing where I'm going. You see, it's a long time since I was last here and I don't want to miss anything."

He nodded with a quaint grown-up air as if he understood and then with that casual manner which children often assume, believing that all adults know exactly what they are talking about, he said,

"Sarah doesn't like the wind and she wouldn't come up here. But Daddy likes standing up here."

Lisa looked round the deck. There was no one else there.

12

Then she looked down at the boy again and thought that if she had a child like him, so fair and beautiful, she wouldn't let him wander about on the top deck of a ferry boat in bad weather because he might slip between the railings and fall overboard.

"Where's your mummy?" she asked, thinking she might take him to his parents.

"In Tasmania," he said carelessly. "We left her there."

Lisa felt a little deflated by his answer, but persisted,

"Isn't anyone travelling with you?"

"Yes, Daddy is. He's in the bar with Sandy. They're drinking whisky. I've just been to peep at them. Sarah's there too. I haven't seen her before. She's very pretty. Yesterday I saw Santa Claus in a big shop in Glasgow." He looked round the deck and then leaned closer to whisper, "I don't think he was really Santa Claus. I think it was someone dressed up to look like him. I pretend I believe in Santa Claus because Daddy likes creeping into my bedroom on Christmas Eve to leave presents on my bed."

Having made this important confidence he gazed at her solemnly for another minute, all the time licking his lollipop. Then he gave her another sweet smile and said,

"I can see you're not a witch. You're too pretty. 'Bye!"

He went scampering across the deck to the companionway and disappeared again and Lisa was left to wonder about a father who liked playing at being Santa Claus yet who preferred to drink whisky in the bar of a ferry boat with a pretty woman, leaving his child to wander about unattended.

But her thoughts did not linger long with the unknown parents of her recent companion because the ferry boat was entering the strait of water, an arrow of wind-ruffled grey pointing the way between the pale sage green slopes of the island and the bracken-covered shores of the mainland.

With a quiver of delight she recognised certain landmarks. There was the big white house, gracious and serene, set back from a small beach of yellow sand overlooking sweeping lawns and backed by the tawny brown of deciduous trees and the

13

bottle green of conifers. There, on the other side, was the small grey church with its tiny pointed steeple, crouching close to the shore.

As the strait grew narrower and the hills crowded closer she noticed the wind did not buffet her so much because its full strength was cut off by the land. The speed of the ferry boat slowed. Ahead four small islands appeared blobs of burnt sienna brown in a swirling mass of grey water. They divided the kyle into two passages and Lisa recalled having visited one of them with her mother to see the remains of a vitrified fort which had been revealed by an archaeological dig which had been taking place when she had last visited her aunt. She knew that the whole area was a historian's delight because so many battles had been fought there from earliest times right up to the seventeenth century.

The ferry boat took the northern passage, passing close to one of the islands on which a red and white beacon was situated. Once through the dangerously narrow passage the boat turned southwards and there opening before it was the western part of the strait gradually widening between dark masses of land, a pathway to the blurred distant horizon.

Picking up speed, the ferry chugged fussily over to the west side of the kyle where granite cliffs topped by wind-bent Scots pines overhung the water. Eventually the cliffs gave way to a wide bay around the edge of which houses huddled to form the village of Ardmont.

Lisa remembered the village as a place of white and colour-washed cottages and stately Victorian villas which had twinkled in the sunlight of early summer, bright amongst the green foliage of trees and shrubs. But now all the houses were a uniform grey and looked as if they were about to be pushed into the water by the sodden brown moors which stretched behind them up to the granite crags of the mountains.

As the ferry approached the long snout of pier thrusting out into the strait, she hurried down to the main deck to find the embarkation gate. She stood near it watching the members of the ferry's crew throwing warps and expertly tying the ferry to

14

the pier before they pushed out the gangway and allowed passengers ashore.

"Good afternoon. Am I right in thinking I'm addressing Miss Elisabeth Roy Smith?" said a man's voice nearby. It was a soft, pleasantly-modulated voice and pronounced the letter "r" with that rolling sound peculiar to the Scots.

Lisa turned to look in surprise at a tall thin man, with smiling grey eyes and sand-coloured wispy hair, who stood beside her.

"Yes, I'm Lisa Smith," she replied.

He held out a long-fingered hand.

"I'm Sandy Lewis. My parents are friends of your aunt's. You probably don't remember, but we met briefly when you came with your mother a few years ago." The grey glance swept over her admiringly. "There have been few changes in us both since then," he added with a hesitant but charming smile.

"Of course I remember you," said Lisa, placing her hand in his. "Your father has a sheep farm and you were full of ideas about resurrecting the old weaving industry to make tweed out of locally produced wool."

Pleasure glinted in his eyes as he responded to her sincere interest.

"That's right. You might be interested to know that I managed to put my ideas into practice. We're actually producing a good quality tweed. I'm just back from Glasgow where I've been trying to make new contacts for selling the stuff. Dad will be here to meet me and, I expect, to meet you too. He rang me up last night to tell me you'd be on this boat and to look out for you. Unfortunately I didn't." His grin was a little sheepish. "I was detained by an old friend."

"In the bar?" suggested Lisa dryly.

His thick sand-coloured eyebrows shot up in surprise.

"How do you know? I didn't see you in there."

"I wasn't. But a small elf in a navy blue duffle coat informed that his daddy was in the bar drinking with someone called Sandy."

15

"Och, that would be wee Johnnie Lamont. How did he come to be talking to you?"

"He thought I was a witch."

"The wee devil!"

"Oh, I didn't mind, but I was rather concerned about him wandering about on his own on the top deck in that wind as we crossed the Firth. He's so small. He could easily have slipped overboard."

"I suppose you're right. Fraser lets him do pretty much as he likes. Here, let me take your bags. I can see Dad over there by the family town carriage."

Lisa looked in the direction he was pointing. A tall man wearing a burberry coat and tweed hat was pacing beside an extremely well-preserved elderly Daimler car.

"You go over to him and I'll follow with your luggage," instructed Sandy.

She did as she was told and was soon shaking hands with Hugh Lewis, who had the same grey eyes as his son set under fierce sandy-coloured eyebrows. His hair, however, which showed below the edge of the greenish tweed hat, was white.

"Och, I'm glad ye've found each other. That's fine, just fine," he boomed. "Ye've fairly grown, Elisabeth, since I last saw ye. Sorry I was to be hearing about Barbara's death. Aye, but ye're her spitting image, only a few inches taller. And I'm thinking ye've a look of Maud about ye too. Ye haven't got that determined tilt to your chin for nothing. Come away with ye and sit in the front with me. Maud's waiting for us. We've been promised tea and some of her home-baked drop scones for doing this wee service, Sandy."

"Good," replied Sandy, who had been putting Lisa's cases in the boot of the car. "Shall I drive?"

"Ach, no. Ye can sit in the back and listen to Elisabeth and me talking."

"I'm glad to hear that Aunt Maud is able to do some baking," said Lisa, as the car turned right on to the road which wound beside the shore. "I was expecting to find her unable to get about."

16

"Well, she canna' do much and she has to take great care. Maisie Weir goes out every morning to give her a hand and to clean through the house, and of course the district nurse and the doctor both call on her regularly."

"Move over to the left, Dad," warned Sandy quietly. "You're out in the middle of the road."

"It's my road, isn't it?" barked the older man, and Sandy laughed.

"That's the way country people talk around here, Lisa," he explained. "They drive in the middle of the road because they're convinced no one else is going to be using it. It can be quite unnerving after driving in the city amongst law-abiding citizens."

"You hold your tongue, lad," retorted Hugh Lewis. "I helped to pay for this road, so it's mine."

Nothing had changed, thought Lisa, looking out at the neat privet hedges which marked the limits of the gardens of the Victorian houses to her left. The road was still hardly the width of two cars.

From behind came the sound of a car's horn.

"Here he comes," murmured Sandy. "I told you to move over." Hugh Lewis made no effort to swing the steering wheel but kept the car in the centre of the road. Glancing at his face, Lisa saw that it was stiff with pride and that there was a wicked blaze in his eyes when they glanced at the rear view mirror.

"Damned arrogance!" he muttered, as the car behind hooted again. "Thinks he owns the place!"

The driver of the car behind sounded its horn again and Lisa turned curiously to look past Sandy through the rear window. All she could see was the top of a black car which was so close to the Daimler that if the big car should stop suddenly there would be a crash.

"Well, since he bought that row of cottages at the back you have to admit he does own a sizeable portion of the village," Sandy was saying mildly. "He was telling me when we were having a drink on the ferry that he'd like to buy The Moorings."

17

The car hooted again and it seemed to Lisa that the sound was derisive.

"Come on, Dad, move over," Sandy said impatiently. "Stop being so stubborn. If you don't he'll take a chance and move out, and heaven knows what might happen."

"Let him, and good riddance," growled the older man stubbornly. Glancing out beyond him, Lisa could see why Sandy was worried. The road ran close to the shore and any car overtaking at speed might run off the road on to the muddy beach.

"But he has the boy ... and ... Sarah with him," persisted Sandy.

"Humph, has he now?" remarked Hugh, with another eagle glance at the mirror. "What's she doing here?"

"She's divorced her husband and has come to live at home for a while." Sandy's voice was flat and dull. Lisa looked at him sharply. His mouth was grim and there was an expression of sadness in his eyes.

"All right, I'll get out of his way," grumbled Hugh suddenly, "but mind you, it's only because he has the child with him. The poor wee laddie can't help having a delinquent parent."

He turned the steering wheel and guided the car closer to the hedges. The car behind accelerated and passed them with an acknowledging hoot on its horn. Lisa saw a boy's face at the front side window and beyond it the bulk of a man's body, had a brief glimpse of the perfectly-chiselled profile of a woman sitting in the back of the car, and then it was past and bumping down the road in front, careering along as if furies were after it.

"Drives too fast, too," muttered Hugh Lewis.

"What do you mean by delinquent?" asked Sandy. "Seems to me Fraser does his best to look after the child with little or no help from anyone around here," objected Sandy.

"There's many a woman would be glad to help mind the child if he weren't so difficult and if his father were less arrogant," snorted Hugh. "What's he want The Moorings for?"

18

"Well, the Morrisons don't want it, you can be sure of that. George has been wanting to sell for some time. He needs to get away to a drier climate, he says. Fraser thinks it's time Ardmont had a decent hotel, so he's thinking of buying the place, converting it and putting a manager in."

"Damned interloper," grumbled Hugh Lewis. "Coming here and turning the place upside down, thinking he can put people out of their homes just to serve his own ends."

"Now, Dad, that's going too far. You can't call him an interloper. After all, he was born here and his family have been building boats here for generations. As for selfish ends, it seems to me he's helping the community as much as himself. The output from the yard has doubled since he took it over. He's employing more men. He tells me he has thirty working there this winter, some of them incomers admittedly. But the yard has given the village new life when it was in danger of becoming a place where only old people lived. As a matter of fact it's helped my business considerably. Yachtsmen's wives often have money to spend and they like local produce."

"By buying you a drink he seems to have bought your loyalty too," jeered Hugh. "I'd no idea you were so friendly with him."

"Fraser bought my loyalty a long time ago," said Sandy quietly. "You can hardly expect me to ignore someone with whom I went to school and who once rescued me from drowning down at the Point."

"Humph, I'd forgotten that."

"I thought you had," said Sandy dryly. Then turning to Lisa he said with a grin, "Take no notice of our bickering, Lisa. I like your cloak."

"I designed and made it myself."

"It would look good in one of our tweeds."

She flashed him an interested glance. For all he was so quiet and self-effacing he had the same stubbornness as his father and she liked the way he had defended the man who had once saved his life.

"I'll take you up on that," she said. "When can I see some tweeds?"

"Any time. Come to the mill some day and see the wool being dyed and spun."

"I'd like to see it being woven too, if I may. For the last two years I've been designing clothes for a fashion house in Manchester and I'm interested in all sorts of fabrics."

A shrewd gleam lit his grey eyes.

"Then you might be just the person I've been looking for," he murmured. "Here we are at the Roy ancestral home."

They had reached the end of the village. Ahead loomed the grey sheds of the boatyard and beyond them loomed the cliffs. Hugh Lewis swung the car out into the middle of the road in order to spike the entrance to a narrow rough road which rose steeply on the left leading to the tall grey house set back from the main road. The car took the hill reluctantly, puffing and panting, its wheels churning over granite chips, and eventually came to a gasping stop beside a small iron gate set in a stone wall.

"You go on to the house and we'll bring the luggage," said Hugh, and needing no second urging Lisa swung out of the car, opened the gate and walked along the red gravel path to the glass-panelled front door of the house. She rang the bell and then turned to look at the view from the doorstep.

It had changed. No longer was it possible to see up the kyle as far as the narrows. A big grey shed adjacent to the narrow road effectively blocked any view to the north. However, it was still possible to look right down the sloping garden to the shore road and beyond that to the kyle and the green hills of the island of Boag sloping down to the curve of Black Rock bay. Nothing had been built as yet on the land below the shore road.

Glancing at the big shed again, Lisa realised at last who had been harassing her Aunt Maud, and who wanted to buy Breck House. He was the same man whose arrogance and impudence aggravated Hugh Lewis, who had once saved Sandy from being drowned. He was Fraser Lamont, boat-builder and the delinquent parent of the child she had met on the ferry.

The door behind her opened and she turned to find her aunt standing there. A tall gaunt woman in her late seventies, Maud Roy was dressed in a tartan skirt and green jumper, and she was leaning on a knobbly walking stick. Her long-jawed, rather austere face softened into a smile and her deep-set brown eyes lit up when she saw Lisa, although she made no gesture of affection.

"Ach, so you're here at last. Aye, it's a bonny face ye have, but you're o'er-thin for my liking," she said abruptly in a harsh voice. "But they tell me it's the fashion to be lean."

She glanced along the path. Sandy and his father were coming with Lisa's cases.

"It's grand to see you, Sandy," called Aunt Maud. "It's a long time since ye came visiting. Come away in. The kettle is on and the scones are buttered."

The view outside might have changed, but inside the house was the same. As she entered the big sitting room Lisa noticed with pleasure the familiar pieces of furniture; the huge mahogany sideboard on which the platters and chafing dishes belonging to an antique silver dinner service glinted in the light from the fire which leapt with orange and blue flames in the cavernous fireplace. Before the fire was a table formed by a Benares brass tray set on top of carved legs and on the mantelpiece above the fireplace blue and white Chinese ginger jars held pride of place. In one corner of the room there was the same corner cupboard containing odds and ends of ivory, small china figurines and tiny silver spoons and salt cellars. And at the big bay window the same starched long lace curtains hung crisp and white.

Sandy and his father stayed for an hour drinking tea, devouring buttered scones and exchanging gossip and wisecracks with Aunt Maud. As they left Sandy extracted a promise from Lisa that she would ring him up as soon as she found time to go and see the mill. Overhearing him, Aunt Maud was enthusiastic about the idea.

"That sounds grand, Sandy. If you can interest the lass in

something maybe she'll stay longer than the month she's promised to me and then yon rascal will realise I mean what I say when I tell him I can't sell this place to him because there's a Roy to follow me."

"So that's how you've been keeping him at bay," remarked Sandy.

"Aye, but I have a feeling in my bones he's going to get the better of me one day by building on that land beyond the road. It's an ideal place for another slipway."

"But surely ye can claim ancient lights," said Hugh Lewis angrily. "Damned if I'd let him get away with it."

"I've tried," said Aunt Maud a little wearily. "I asked my lawyer, Murdo Menzies, to write to him. A lot of good that did! I had a visit from the Town and Country planning people. They told me that as long as the building doesn't take any light from my windows I can't claim anything. It's too far away from me to do that."

"Looks as if he's trying to squeeze you out," said Hugh.

"Over my dead body," replied Aunt Maud grimly, "and not even then."

Later when the long red velvet curtains covered the lace ones and made a semi-circle of warm colour at one end of the sitting room blotting out the dark windy December night, and the firelight leapt cosily illuminating Aunt Maud's fine-featured, angular face, Lisa learned more about her aunt's fight to keep Breck House.

"I've had many fights in my time, Lisa, to keep my independence, my house and my land, and I've won all of them. But I'm getting old and this struggle has taxed my strength. Yon man is young and tough, and for all he has the charm of the devil, he's as hard as nails."

"But who is he and where has he come from? Mr. Lewis says he's an interloper, but Sandy says he was born here and went to school with him," said Lisa.

"He's a Lamont, and that family have lived in this place for generations. Boatbuilders all of them, sometimes successful, sometimes not. This one's father, Charlie Lamont, was un-

22

successful. He was no businessman and was near to bankruptcy when he was drowned."

"How did that happen?"

"An accident when he was taking a yacht out to its mooring. The boom swung over, hit him on the head and he fell overboard. He sank like a stone. Fraser was twelve at the time. His mother sold the yard to a syndicate of Glasgow businessmen who were interested in yachting. She took Fraser and his sister Anna to live near her own people in Glasgow. I'm thinking it was enough to break the boy's heart taking him away from her, from the home and the boats he loved. But I've since discovered he couldn't possibly have had a heart to break."

"When did he come back?" asked Lisa. "He wasn't here when Mother and I visited you."

"No, he wasn't. He came back five years ago from heaven knows where, bringing the boy with him. He says the lad is his son and they tell me there's a family likeness. No sign of a mother. It seems that when he left school Fraser was apprenticed to boatbuilding and when he'd finished his apprenticeship he emigrated to Hobart in Tasmania, a great yachting place, so I believe."

"Do you know why he came back?"

"For all I dislike the man I'm willing to suggest that it was the pull of his homeland that brought him. Anyway, he had money and had no difficulty in buying the yard back. It had changed hands several times in recent years. No one had been able to make a success of it partly because of bad management and partly because of lack of local knowledge."

"Judging by the new sheds and his desire to buy Breck House, I gather Mr. Lamont has been successful," observed Lisa.

"Aye. From the moment he arrived he talked of nothing but expansion, of wanting to build more boats and store more boats. He knows his business all right. He's clever at designing and during the past few years he's built up a clientele of wealthy business men. But he can't extend to the north and west of his property because of the cliffs. There's only one way, and that's why he wants my land. Three times he's come and offered to buy me out and three times I've refused. Last time was hard because I'd been very ill and I was tired. But I kept thinking of all the Roys who had lived on this land and I kept thinking of you and I couldn't agree. So he said he'd try and get permission to build on the land beyond the road."

Lisa frowned into the fire.

"Who owns the property to the west of you?" she asked.

"That's the Morrisons' guest house. It's called The Moorings."

"Sandy told me that the Morrisons want to sell it and Mr. Lamont is thinking of buying it and converting it into a hotel."

Aunt Maud's face registered shock which was followed quickly by anger.

"The devil!" she hissed. "The wily devil. So he'd box me in! As if he didn't own enough property in this village. He bought the row of cottages on the other side of The Moorings so that he could offer accommodation to anyone coming to work for him. Ach, how can I stop him from boxing me in like that?"

She leaned back in her chair, her eyes closed and her face drawn with pain. Lisa watched her anxiously, trying to think of a way in which to help.

"He'll get it," muttered Aunt Maud. "Who else would have the money available around here to buy the place and convert it? Somehow we must stop him, Lisa."

"Have you any money?" asked Lisa.

Aunt Maud opened her eyes, surprised at being asked such a direct and rather impertinent question by the young woman sitting opposite to her whose hair glowed with copper sheen in the firelight and whose wide-set eyes danced and glittered with life.

"A little," she replied. "Why do you want to know?"

"Have you enough to buy The Moorings?"

"I doubt it. I should think the Morrisons will want a good price. Yon rascal will give it to them."

24

"Where did Fraser Lamont get his money?"

"There's one story going around that he married for money out in Tasmania, and that when his wife died she left him everything she had inherited from her grandmother."

"How convenient for him that she should die," observed Lisa dryly, who was disliking Fraser Lamont more and more. "If you like I could ask Daddy to lend me the money to buy the place."

"But what would you do with it?"

"I could continue to run it as a guesthouse or like Mr. Lamont I could turn it into the good hotel he seems to think Ardmont requires. Why should he get all the profit?"

Aunt Maud stared at her and then her brown eyes began to twinkle and she started to laugh, and before long she and Lisa were laughing together.

"Ach, Lisa, you're a lass after my own heart and I think I knew that when I wrote to you. I was feeling so low, lower than I've ever felt in my whole life, when I learned that I could do nothing to stop him from building in front of me if he wanted to. I felt sorry for myself, thinking I had no one to turn to. But now you're here and I'm beginning to feel better. I haven't laughed like that for years," said Aunt Maud.

"I'm glad you feel better. Together we'll show Mr. Lamont we Roy women aren't to be treated lightly. Anything he can do we can do better. Would you like me to write to Daddy?"

"Not yet. I've another idea at the back of my mind which might work. I'll have to have a word with George Morrison, though. We'll invite him over one evening for a drop of whisky. There's nothing George likes better than a drop of the malt."

When she had seen her aunt to bed Lisa went to the small bedroom which had been her mother's. Strangely enough it had none of the charm which it had possessed those long summer evenings over six years ago. Now it seemed cold and austere and she was glad that there was an electric convector heater she could put on to warm the chilly air and that someone had thoughtfully switched on the electric blanket in the bed.

Snuggling down into the warmth listening to wind howling round the house shaking the window and clattering the slates on the roof, she thought back over the day's events; of Johnnie Lamont with his sweet smile and big blue eyes, neglected and ignored by his father who had preferred to drink whisky with Sandy and a certain Lady Sarah. Who was Sarah? She had meant to ask Aunt Maud, but they had been so busy planning ways in which they could foil Fraser Lamont in his attempt to buy The Moorings that she had forgotten to ask.

Lisa yawned suddenly and turned over on her side. Delicious waves of drowsiness swept over her. The buffeting of the wind and the sea air had both made her sleepy and she had no desire to lie awake puzzling over the identity of a woman she had never met, but as she drifted off to sleep the last image which flashed across the dark inner screen of her closed eyelids was of Sandy Lewis's face set in lines of sadness when he had mentioned that Sarah had divorced her husband.

CHAPTER II

CLEAR sparkling mornings with the kyle a ribbon of blue satin contrasting with the bleached winter-rimed grass of the island of Boag. Calm sunny afternoons with the distant mountains lavender-coloured, their summits iced with white. Deep purple gloamings after an orange sun had slipped below the horizon. So day followed day during Lisa's first two weeks as an anti-cyclone brought a cold fine spell of weather to the district.

Contrary to her expectations she did not find time heavy on her hands. There were Aunt Maud's two dogs to be walked three times a day, a chore which Lisa enjoyed because it gave her the opportunity to explore the countryside and the village again. Since Aunt Maud did not rise until midday Lisa also had the chance to try her hand at housekeeping and at cooking, both of which activities she had always left to Mandy when she had lived in Manchester. Admittedly Mrs. Weir still came to do the heavy work once a week, but there were still beds to make, washing to do and dusting, and although she found that sort of work dull she enjoyed cooking because it was creative.

She also enjoyed shopping in the village and it was one day when she was in the village general store that she met Mrs. Morrison for the first time.

The weather had changed and it was pouring with rain so she had gone to the shop in Aunt Maud's small car. In the store she waited for Mrs. Ferguson, the proprietress, to serve the woman before her, half listening to the conversation which was taking place as she looked round the crowded shelves.

"There you are Mrs. Morrison, that's you," said Mrs. Ferguson as she packed a final purchase into the woman's shopping basket. "Ach, it's terrible morning."

27

"It is so. And I'm having to walk – the car's out of action. Good thing our Gavin is home."

"When did he come?"

"Yesterday. He'll be here until after Hogmanay."

"Aye, it's fine to be a schoolteacher with those long holidays. Is Marjorie home too?"

"No. She's better off where she is. Well, I'll be on my way."

Lisa made her few purchases and hurried out of the shop to the car. Soon she was driving along the shore road, windscreen wipers clacking noisily, tyres swishing. Ahead of her she could see the robust figure of Mrs. Morrison. It did not take long to overtake her and to pull into the side of the road. As the woman approached the car Lisa reached over and opened the door and called out,

"Can I give you a lift? I'm going to Breck House."

"That's very kind of you, miss."

Mrs. Morrison showed no hesitation about getting into the car and dumped her shopping basket on the back seat before she settled down in the seat next to Lisa.

"You're Miss Roy's niece," she observed chattily. "I've seen you out walking the dogs and George my husband told me he met you when he was over seeing her the other day. How is she keeping?"

"She's up and down, sometimes well and like her old self and sometimes very poorly," replied Lisa.

Mrs. Morrison nodded her head sagely as she loosened her wet headscarf.

"Aye, that's how it will be for her, poor soul. She'll be glad to have you with her, one of her own kin. There's no one like your own kin when you're in trouble or ill," and observing that she had a sympathetic listener Mrs. Morrison launched into a recital of how many times she had found her "own kin" had stood by her in time of trouble, finishing by quoting the example of her daughter Marjorie who had been found a job by her uncle in Glasgow when living in Ardmont had become too much for her.

28

By that time they had reached The Moorings, a big sprawling house built of grey granite, and Lisa had not been able to say a word. As Mrs. Morrison took her basket from the back seat, however, Lisa slipped in an innocuous question.

"I hear you and your husband would like to leave Ardmont too. Have you had any more offers for the guesthouse?"

"No. Only the one. A good offer too, but George isn't keen to sell to Mr. Lamont for some reason. He doesn't care for him ... not since Marjorie ..." She broke off abruptly, then started again, "But as I say to him, what has liking a person got to do with selling a place? If I could have my own way I'd sell it to Fraser Lamont tomorrow. As it is I can see us waiting for years for another good offer."

"How much are you asking for it?" asked Lisa bluntly.

"Fraser has offered fifteen thousand pounds. I won't let George sell for less, you can mark my words. Well, thank you again, Miss Smith. Give my regards to Miss Roy, and season's greetings to ye both."

Fifteen thousand pounds! Fraser Lamont must be flush with money if he was able to offer that much for a dilapidated guesthouse. Either that or his credit must be good, thought Lisa as she garaged the car and made her way through the slanting rain to the house. There had been no time to ask Mrs. Morrison why George Morrison did not like Fraser Lamont. And then there had been that curious remark about her daughter Marjorie.

Where would she find out about Marjorie Morrison? She decided she would ask Sandy when she saw him that afternoon when she went to see the mill. Maybe she would ask him about Lady Sarah, too.

Ardmont Mill consisted of two big asbestos sheds. In one shed were the carding machines run by electricity into which the dyed wool was fed to be prepared ready for spinning. As always fascinated by the change brought about in the fibre by the action of carding and spinning, Lisa watched the virgin wool, dyed, golden yellow, emerald green, emerge as long single threads of yarn ready to be sent to the weavers.

"What lovely colours," she murmured. "Where do you get the dyes?"

"Some of them are vegetable dyes just as were used in the old days," explained Sandy. "For instance, the root of the iris plant makes pale yellow, bog myrtle this deeper gold. Heather tips give a light green, and crotal, which is a rock lichen and which grows only in clear, unpolluted air, makes a rusty orange. Of course we use synthetic dyes as well, especially in the winter when the dye plants can't be gathered."

"Who weaves the tweed?"

"The villagers in their own homes. My mother is a weaver. In fact it was seeing her carrying on the traditional industry of the area spinning on a foot-driven spinning wheel and using the hand loom that made me think of reviving the industry as a cottage industry which might keep villagers from moving away to the towns. Dad lent me some money and I received a Government grant to build the sheds and erect the machinery. I persuaded some of the older women of the village to get out their looms and so we started. Gradually we've been able to replace the old hand-looms with modern steel foot-powered looms which go faster. Now we have thirty weavers of both sexes and several apprentices amongst the young school leavers."

"What's their rate of production?"

"In a week a good weaver will produce two to two and a half tweeds, that is a strip of cloth eight yards long by twenty-eight inches wide."

"You must feel very pleased to think you've achieved so much in such a short time?"

"It's nice of you to say so," replied Sandy with his charming diffident smile. "But there's something lacking. We don't sell as much as we should. I feel our tweeds could be as well-known as the Harris or Bute tweeds. I was hoping they would put Ardmont on the map again as a tweed-producing centre. I know what I'm doing when it comes to spinning and weaving, but I don't seem to have the knack of selling. No gift of the gab, I suppose," he added, his smile becoming self-disparaging.

"We'll go up to the farmhouse now. I'd like you to meet my mother and to show you some tweed she's just woven. I'm hoping you'll accept a length of it to make a cloak to your own design."

The Lewis farmhouse was built on a grassy knoll and commanded a fine view of the widening kyle as it flowed south. It was an old house and possessed fine examples of mullioned windows, stone vertical bars dividing the panes of glass. At the back of the house a big room acted as a studio where Mrs. Lewis worked at her loom, watching the shuttle as it shot back and forth automatically. She stopped when she saw Lisa enter the room with Sandy and came forward to be introduced.

"Sandy tells me you're a dress designer," she said. "I'd like your opinion of this tweed I've just finished. D'ye think the blend of colours is right or are they all too positive?"

Lisa lifted some of the cloth in her hand. It was light and yet firm and possessed a faint sheen. The colours were her own. There were the burning bronze and the glinting green so aptly described by Sandy combined with a brilliant yellow in a traditional check pattern. As a cloak for herself it would be perfect.

"They are positive," she agreed. "But on the right person it'll look great." With a quick twitch she released more of the cloth from its roll and draped it round herself. "Worn as a coat or a cloak with the right accessories it would be perfect."

Sandy and his mother stared. The colour of Lisa's hair and eyes seemed to be intensified by the colours of the tweed.

"You're right," said Sandy. "It's perfect."

"If only –" began Mrs. Lewis, and stopped short.

"If only what?" he demanded, turning on her as if expecting her to disagree with him.

"I was thinking how wonderful it would be if Lisa could design a suit to be made out of one of our tweeds and model it for an advertisement to go into one of the Scottish magazines. It would be grand publicity."

Touched by the softly-spoken suggestion, Lisa smiled as she tossed the tweed back on to the table.

"I could certainly design something, but as for modelling, you'd be better with someone who is trained and possibly well-known."

"Like Sarah," said Sandy quietly, and his mother gave him a sharp worried glance.

"Who is she?" asked Lisa.

"Lady Popham. She was Sarah Chisholm before she married Sir Jack Popham. You may have heard of her," replied Sandy.

"Yes, I have. I've seen and admired her photograph many times. Do you know her?"

"Her parents came to live at Creddon Hall at the top of Loch Creddon about ten years ago," offered Mrs. Lewis when her son seemed disinclined to answer Lisa. "That reminds me, Sandy, did Fraser tell you that Mr. Chisholm wants him to do the alterations on the big yacht he's bought?"

"It was on that basis that Sarah introduced herself to Fraser in the bar on the ferry," replied Sandy.

"D'ye mean to say she didn't know him already?"

"You seem to have forgotten that Sarah hasn't been in Ardmont for almost eight years," snapped Sandy impatiently, "and she's only returned now because she isn't wanted elsewhere."

"Is it as long as that?" murmured Mrs. Lewis placidly. "My, how time flies, and now it's time for tea. Ye won't mind having it in the kitchen, will ye, Lisa? Hughie will be in from the barn and he'll be wanting to have a wee crack with ye about Maud."

It was almost an hour later before Lisa had Sandy to herself again and that was only for a few minutes when she was leaving. It was still raining and she asked him to sit next to her in the car.

When he raised his eyebrows in surprise she giggled and murmured,

"Don't look so astounded and shocked. I only want to ask you a question. It wasn't possible in there with your parents present."

His surprise vanished as understanding dawned and he slid into the seat beside her and shut the car door.

"Now you've roused my curiosity," he said. "What do you want to know?"

"Why did Marjorie Morrison leave Ardmont, and why does George Morrison dislike Fraser Lamont?"

Sandy gave a low whistle.

"The answer to that is rather spicy, and I'm glad you've asked me and not some busybody from the village, because probably the story I'm going to tell you isn't at all true."

"Why isn't it true?"

"Because Marjorie Morrison happens to be one of the biggest prevaricators I've ever come across."

"Well, come on, tell me. What is she *supposed* to have done?"

"It isn't a case of what she's supposed to have done, it's what she said Fraser did. You see when he came back from Tasmania Johnnie was not quite two and still needed looking after during the day. Marjorie had left school a year earlier but had done nothing very productive except to work as a waitress in the guesthouse during the summer months. So when Fraser asked around for someone to mind his child Marjorie was pushed forward by her mother, thinking it would be suitable employment for the girl."

"Did he employ her?"

"Yes, for three months. Then suddenly he gave her the sack."

"Why?"

"Being Fraser he never told anyone why. He just told her to clear out and he brought in an older woman to live in and be housekeeper and baby-sitter."

"What did Marjorie do then?"

"Well, her father gave Fraser hell but returned home, so I've been told, a very chastened man having been told a few home-truths about his daughter. For a while all was quiet and then the rumour, a very ugly one began to spread. It had its origin, as you might guess, with Marjorie who told someone

33

who told someone else, and so on, that while she had been working for him Fraser had made several passes at her and had also made what she considered to be improper suggestions. She made out that he had sacked her because she had refused to comply with that suggestion."

"And you didn't believe her story."

Sandy shook his head.

"Not on your life. Nor would you have done if you'd known Marjorie. Nor will you when you meet Fraser."

However, it was some time before Lisa met Fraser Lamont and was able to judge for herself what sort of a person he was. Meanwhile she built up an image of him based on the opinion of Aunt Maud only slightly modified by what she had learned from Sandy and from the boy she had met on the ferry boat. She imagined him to a burly granite-faced individual with an overbearing manner who went his own way regardless of others.

One day after Christmas, she was returning from her afternoon walk with the dogs when her attention was caught by a movement on the narrow shore. The two red setters also noticing the movement began to bark and strain at their leashes, pulling her across the road in the direction of the shore.

At once she saw that two boys were attacking a third smaller boy and even as she watched one of them flung the small boy to the ground, squatted on top of him and taking him by the shoulders began to bang his head against the ground. Shocked and sickened by such violence, Lisa stood stock still as she saw blond floppy hair bounce up and down on the small boy's head.

Then she burst into action. Sensing her anger, the dogs bounded forward yelping and snarling. The two bigger boys looked round, stood up and ran off. Lisa shouted after them but doubted if they heard her because of the noise of the barking setters.

Quickly she knelt beside the blond-haired boy who was struggling to his feet. She recognised the dark blue duffle coat and the dark eyes, which gazed up at her solemnly. His face was grazed and he had the beginnings of a black eye.

"They thought you were a witch," he said. "That's why they ran."

"Who were they?"

"Doug Pettigrew and Jimmy Fox."

"Why were they fighting with you?"

"They called Daddy a rude name, so I punched them, and then they began to punch me."

"But they're bigger and older than you."

"I know."

"Then why did you punch them?"

"I told you. They called Daddy a name. They'd no right to do that because he isn't what they said. I know." His blue eyes filled suddenly with tears which he tried in vain to brush away with dirty grazed knuckles. "They hurt me," he blubbered, and Lisa lost her heart for the first time in her life to a seven-year-old boy.

When he was a little calmer and had accepted the use of her handkerchief he agreed to let her walk home with him to find his father.

"He won't be in the house," he explained, waving his hand in the direction of the comfortable whitewashed villa which was situated in the rising ground at the back of the boatyard, surrounded by an untidy garden. "He might be in the office, or in one of the sheds. My name is Johnnie."

"And mine is Lisa."

"He might be a bit cross 'cos I've been in another fight, so you won't mind if I keep holding your hand, will you, Lisa?"

"No, I won't," she replied, squeezing the hand in question, while in her mind she rehearsed the short sharp reprimand she was going to give Fraser Lamont when she met him concerning the welfare of his son.

Passing the canvas-covered yachts laid up for the winter, they crossed the muddy boatyard to a fairly modern wooden building. Johnnie opened the door and they went into a room furnished as an office on the walls of which the plans of various yachts were pinned. At a desk sat a middle-aged woman

35

typing. When she saw Johnnie and Lisa she peered over the top of her spectacles and said,

"Ach, what have ye been up to now?"

"He's been in a fight," drawled Lisa in her haughtiest manner. "And I've brought him home. Would you please tell me where I can find Mr. Lamont?"

The woman stared at her severely.

"Ach, I canna be disturbing him now. He's talking to a very important customer. Leave the bairn here with me. He'll be all right."

"I'll do nothing of the sort. What I have to say to Mr. Lamont is just as important as his customer, so I wish to see him personally," retorted Lisa, conscious of a draught on the back of her legs, knowing that the outer door of the office had opened behind her and that someone had entered.

"Then you shall be seeing him personally in a few minutes," said a man's voice behind her, a voice through which a thread of laughter ran, tantalising and elusive. "Jeannie, will you please show Miss Smith into the other office? I won't be long."

Lisa whirled quickly, but she was not quick enough. The door banged shut as he stepped outside again. Going to the window, all she could see of him was the back of his square-shouldered figure as he bent to speak to someone in the driving seat of an expensive-looking car.

Johnnie tugged at her hand.

"That was Daddy," he whispered. "We'd better do as he says."

Lisa turned and caught the tail-end of a superior smile on Jeannie's face as she stood up, opened the door to the inner office and simpered,

"This way, please, Miss Smith."

As she walked past the smirking Jeannie into the other office Lisa could not recall having felt so foolish in her life before. The fact that the man she had come to reprimand personally had recognised her, even though her back had been turned to him, and had called her by her name, when she had no idea what he looked like, made her feel at a disadvantage,

36

which was a new and unpleasant experience.

Anger that he had placed her at a disadvantage swirled in a hot flood through her. She stalked over to the window of the office which looked out over a motley collection of boat-trailers and other yachting equipment. Johnnie, forgetful of the need to hold her hand and seemingly happy to be in his father's office, went to the desk where he began to play with some drawing instruments which had been left there.

Words, critical and disparaging, had formed in Lisa's mind and were ready to be spoken as soon as Fraser Lamont opened the door, and as she heard the sound of his approaching foot-steps through the outer office she tensed ready to attack at once.

The door opened and she spun round to face him. Surprise dispersed her anger momentarily and had the effect of gagging her so that instead of speaking she stared in silence.

Far from being the burly granite-faced individual with the overbearing manner she had imagined, he was handsome, blandly polite, and humour showed in the quirk at the corner of his mouth. About thirty-four years of age, not much taller than herself, he had a compact lithe physique which even his rough working clothes of tough denim pants and dark turtle-necked sweater could not hide. He leaned easily against the closed door and returned her gaze with blue-black eyes which took in every detail of her face.

"Now, what can I do for you, Miss Smith?" he asked plea-santly. Then Johnnie turned to look at him and the dark eyes shifted their glance away from her face to that of the boy. He lunged away from the door to squat before his son and to touch with gentle fingers the purple mark beneath Johnnie's right eye.

"That's a beauty, Johnnie," he murmured. "How did you get it?"

"Doug Pettigrew hit me," replied Johnnie, blinking rap-idly, trying, Lisa guessed, to prevent tears from spilling out again.

"There were two of them, both bigger than he," she interjected quickly. "One of them was lying on top of him gripping his shoulders and banging his head on the ground. When they saw me coming they ran away."

Fraser stood up and faced her. The humour had gone leaving his mouth a straight line above a square determined chin and making his eyes look almost black.

"You interfered," he snapped.

Was he suggesting that she had no right to interfere? Lisa tilted her chin as her original annoyance returned.

"I went to stop it before any serious damage could be done to Johnnie," she snapped back.

He stared at her curiously and consideringly before turning to Johnnie and asking curtly,

"Who started the fight?"

Johnnie looked up at him, his eyelashes fluttering and his lower lip trembling, no doubt wishing that Lisa was holding his hand.

"I did," he quavered. "They called you a rude name, so I punched them."

The man's face softened slightly and humour touched his mouth again as he looked down at the boy.

"It was brave of you to defend me, Johnnie, but try to remember never to get into a fight unless you're sure you can finish it. Both those boys were bigger than you and could have hurt you badly. It was silly of you to take them on. Now, off you run to see Mrs. Dobie up at the house. She'll bathe your wounds and do something about that eye."

Lisa felt her antipathy to the man rising several inches higher when she saw Johnnie's eyes fill with tears and his chin wobble ominously as he cried out,

"But I don't want to go and see Mrs. Dobie! I want to stay with Lisa. She's kind."

"So is Mrs. Dobie."

"No, she isn't, only when you're there. She's rough and she hurts me and she's always saying 'tut, tut.' I hate her!" blurted the boy.

"That's not true, Johnnie." The man's voice was wearily

38

patient as if he'd gone through this scene many times before. Yet the whiplash of authority crackled in it when he added, "Now, go to the house, at once."

Johnnie hesitated, his tearful eyes turning to Lisa hopefully, but in spite of her antipathy to his father she knew enough about dealing with children to realise she must not oppose a parent's authority in front of the child, so she smiled and said,

"Go along, Johnnie. I expect I'll see you again soon. I take the dogs for a walk every afternoon."

His eyes lit up and his tears vanished miraculously and his sweet smile appeared.

"Do you think I could come with you?" he asked.

"Any time you like."

"Johnnie, get going," prompted Fraser sternly.

With a wary glance at his father the boy ran out of the office and through the outer room, banging the door of the building behind him. Fraser closed the inner door on the sound of Jeannie's typing and turned to face Lisa once more.

"Thank you for going to his rescue," he said coldly. "I doubt if your interference was necessary or wise. If he picks a fight he should be prepared to finish it. He has to learn to fight his own battles without assistance from others and also to learn when not to pick fights."

Pride. Oodles of it, thought Lisa with a sudden flash of insight into the character of the man. It was there in the set of his straight shoulders, in the direct glance of his dark eyes and in the hard line of his shapely mouth. Oh, no wonder he and Aunt Maud did not see eye to eye.

But anger was bubbling up again, anger that Johnnie should be made to suffer because of that pride.

"And next time he gets into a fight defending your good name and I happen to be passing, you'd prefer me to walk by on the other side of the road, I suppose," she exclaimed furiously. "Oh, yes, I get the message loud and clear, Mr. Lamont. You brook no interference. But hasn't it occurred to you that Johnnie wouldn't get into a fight if he wasn't neglected and ignored? And if you think he's the sort who can

39

fight to the finish without any help you're going to be very disappointed in him. He isn't like you!"

She knew instantly she had made a mistake because instead of reacting angrily he leaned back against the door, folded his arms across his chest and stared at her with narrowed eyes.

"Isn't he?" he drawled. "You know me so well, then? I find that surprising, because as far as I know this is the first time you and I have met."

His bland insolence prickled under her skin, making her squirm inwardly as she realised that her knowledge of him was based entirely on hearsay and he knew that. But she allowed none of her discomfiture to show and returned his gaze steadily as she replied.

"That's true. This is the first time we've met, yet you knew who I was even when I was standing with my back to you."

Humour was back, softening his mouth, glinting in his eyes.

"I recognised the dogs tied up outside. And surely by now you are aware that every newcomer to the village is discussed in full by the villagers," he explained. "Your knowledge of me, like mine of you, must be based entirely on the opinions of others. Yours, I surmise, is coloured by your aunt's comments, and since there's no love lost between her and me quite naturally her opinion of me is not particularly good."

"Neither is the opinion of a few others," she retorted airily, thinking of Mr. Lewis's forthright comments, and she was pleased to see she had scored a point as his dark eyebrows twitched together in a frown of displeasure.

"How long are you staying in Ardmont?" he asked brusquely, changing the subject abruptly.

"Until Aunt Maud is better," she fenced, not wanting to give anything away.

"She'll never get better. She's dying."

The curt brutality of his statement took her breath away.

"How do you know?" she gasped.

"It's common knowledge. The whole village knows. Do you mean to tell me no one has had the guts to tell you yet? Haven't you seen Doc Clarke?"

"Not yet. He comes tomorrow."

"Then I'd like to suggest to you that you ask him for the truth about her condition. You will probably get a shock, but the truth is often shocking, and that's why people shy away from speaking it," he said coolly. "Why have you chosen this time of the year to come and stay? It's not the usual time for a holiday."

His sharp direct questions and the autocratic way in which he had told her what to do when the doctor called irritated Lisa, but with an effort she controlled her irritation and answered patiently and honestly,

"I came because she wrote and asked me to come. I happened to be free because I hadn't a job. Aunt Maud said she wanted me because I'm the only surviving Roy."

"But your name is Smith," he said sharply.

"It is, but my middle name is Roy, and my mother was the only child of William Roy, Aunt Maud's brother. She used to live at Breck House before she was married."

Horizontal lines creased his forehead as he searched his memory.

"I think I can remember her. She had red hair too," he said. Before she knew what she was doing Lisa was touching the strands of hair which showed below the front of her knitted hat.

"It isn't red," she defended, rising easily to the taunt.

"I expect you have a fancy name for the colour, but it looks like red to me, and Roy means Red in Scotland," he replied imperturbably. "Why hasn't your mother come to see her aunt?"

"She died a few years ago."

"I see." He drawled the words and his eyes narrowed again, the dark lashes almost meeting, hiding any expression. "So when Maud dies you'll expect to inherit Breck House. Is that why you're here, to make sure the will is made in your favour?"

This time she made no attempt to control her temper.

"No, it isn't," she flared. "I had no idea Aunt Maud was

41

dying when I decided to come, and although I know of no reason why I should answer your impertinent questions, Mr. Lamont, I'd like to make it clear that I came because I want to help her, because she's my only living relative on my mother's side and . . ."

"Very commendable," he jeered.

"Oh," she raged, "don't you ever have a kind thought for another person?"

"Not often. In my experience sentiment is a waste of time."

"So everything you do is governed by self-interest," she accused.

"Usually."

She could not be sure, but she thought she saw humour glint again in the depths of his eyes as he answered laconically. However, the expression was so brief and his mouth had not changed, so she decided she had imagined it.

"And I suppose you'll do anything to get what you want," she persisted.

His gaze lingered consideringly on the fronds of red hair, on her glinting hazel eyes and then on her generous passionate mouth, before he murmured,

"Anything."

His cool appraisal combined with the quiet way in which he spoke sent a thrill of alarm through Lisa and for a moment she had a strong sensation of having been caught in a trap from which there was no escape. Somehow she must get away from him out of the trap and into the fresh free air.

"I don't wonder there's no love lost between you and Aunt Maud," she remarked. Then coolly pulling on her gloves and swinging her long scarf over her shoulder she walked towards him. He did not move. Standing before him, tall and slender, her eyes almost on a level with his, she said firmly,

"I don't think we have anything else to say to each other, so I'll leave. Good afternoon, Mr. Lamont."

Still he did not move nor did his gaze waver. She was so close to him she could see a jagged scar on his face below the right cheekbone. It must have been a fairly recent wound because the marks left by the stitches were still very plain.

"I've one more thing to say," he replied smoothly. "I'd rather you didn't encourage Johnnie to go walking with you in the afternoons. There's enough tittle-tattle goes on in the village without you and me providing more food for rumour to thrive on."

"I'm afraid I don't understand," said Lisa stiltedly.

"Once it is known that you and Johnnie are friendly it won't take long for someone to suggest that there's more in your friendship with him than is obvious."

"You mean that someone will think you and I have some sort of clandestine relationship?" she asked, the colour deepening in her cheeks.

"I do. If you were older, middle-aged, I doubt if any suspicions would arise. But as it is you're young and ..." He paused and his gaze flicked over her face again before he continued with an impish grin, "And almost beautiful, in spite of the red hair."

Thoroughly confused by the compliment as well as by the humour, Lisa gaped. Then she remembered what Sandy had told her about Marjorie Morrison. Anger that this man should place her in the same category as a simple-minded adolescent who had probably made a fool of herself by becoming infatuated with her employer chased the colour from her face and made her eyes spark dangerously.

"And so you would deprive Johnnie of a little friendship and companionship just because you're afraid I might make up stories about you?" she hissed.

"You see what I mean? You've been a few weeks in the place and already you know it all," he said, unmoved by her anger. "You're quite right – that is the reason for my concern. I wouldn't want the blame for your loss of reputation to be placed at my door, Miss Red Smith. So stay away from Johnnie, if you please. Good afternoon."

He swung the door open just as the telephone on the desk rang. Without apology he went straight to it and Lisa was left to make her exit unnoticed. As she left the room she heard him saying,

"Hello, Sarah. I was hoping you'd ring. Tell your father I've made all the arrangements and should be in London on New Year's Eve. We could meet . . ."

The door crashed to behind her, helped on its way, she suspected, by a hefty kick from a sea-booted foot.

Head held high, cheeks flaming, Lisa stalked through the outer office wondering how much Jeannie had heard through the thin partition wall. Outside the building she untied the waiting dogs. The sun had already slid behind the hills at the back of the village and the winter twilight was chilly with the promise of a frosty night to come.

As she skirted round the shrouded yachts she spared a quick glance for the lighted front window of the white house where Johnnie would be receiving attention from the rough Mrs. Dobie.

Poor Johnnie! How she wished she could have tended his wounds. He was so much in need of love and attention. Not that she doubted his father loved him in his own fashion, but she guessed that the tough, proud man with whom she had just crossed swords and who had admitted that he thought sentiment to be a waste of time had little time to spare to give Johnnie the care that a mother would give him. He was too busy expanding his business at the expense of other property owners in Ardmont or making arrangements to meet beautiful photographer's model for that, thought Lisa a trifle waspishly.

And yet he had had the nerve to tell her to stay away from Johnnie because he did not want any gossip. As if she cared for gossip! If he thought she was going to do what he had asked and ignore Johnny when she met him out walking then he had underestimated Lisa Roy Smith. She would walk and talk with Johnnie whenever she liked, giving him, she hoped, a little of the love and guidance she thought he needed. No one, not even a man as forceful as Fraser Lamont, could stop her from doing what she considered to be right when she rec-

44

ognised the need of another human being.

Such was her resolve as she returned to Breck House from the boatyard that day, but she had little chance to keep it immediately because Aunt Maud had a slight heart attack and had to be put to bed. Lisa called the doctor and learned from him that Fraser had not been wrong when he had suggested that Aunt Maud was dying. Apparently she had had a severe stroke earlier in the year about which she had not informed Lisa.

"Of course, she might live another couple of years or the next stroke might be a severe one and completely paralyse her or kill her," said the young doctor as he pulled on sea-boots and then put on an oilskin and sou'wester. As most of his practice was spread out along the shores of the kyle and of Loch Creddon he made many of his house-calls by speedboat and his noisy vehicle was a familiar sight on fine days as it roared past the village, sending up fans of spray.

"She'll have to stay in bed until she recovers from this attack. I'll tell Nurse More to look in every day until she's better," he added before he left the house.

Lisa found the plump, pink-cheeked district nurse a welcome visitor. She was always calm and smiling even though she had so many calls to make checking up on the elderly people who were sick as well as on the young babies, and for the first time Lisa realised how dependent on the nurse such people were, especially in an area as remote as the Ardmont peninsula.

Now that she knew the nature of Aunt Maud's illness she was very glad she had been free to come when the old lady had written to her, and for the present she had no intention of leaving Ardmont and returning to Manchester to look for another job. While Aunt Maud needed her she would stay.

CHAPTER III

On New Year's Eve Sandy Lewis called in to ask after Aunt Maud after he had finished working at the mill, and when Lisa told him that she would be staying he looked pleased.

"Your walking out on your boss that day seems to have been fortuitous for me as well as for your aunt," he said as he sipped the tea she had made for him.

"Fortuitous for you? In what way?" asked Lisa, wishing he would be more direct in his approach. She knew he was shy, but there were times when his kid-gloved manner towards her was irritating. He treated her as if she were an article made of delicate porcelain instead of a healthy young woman with a mind of her own.

"Well, I've been thinking," he began diffidently, then added hurriedly, "I hope you won't think I'm pushing Lisa in asking you this . . . and you can refuse, you know."

"Sandy, come to the point," she urged gently. "I'll be the one to decide whether I refuse or not once I know what it is you want me to do."

"The point is . . . I need you," he said in a rush.

"Oh, Sandy!" she gurgled. "This is so sudden!"

"Ach, not in that way," he said testily, not seeing the humour of the situation. "I mean I need your ability and flair for designing clothes, your eye for good colour combinations. That cloak and skirt which you've made from the tweed I gave you shows off the material to advantage. If you would design more outfits like that and we could have made them up and advertised I'm sure our sales of cloth would increase."

"Have you spoken to Sarah Popham yet?" asked Lisa.

His grey glance slid away from hers to the fire and his mouth tightened.

"No," he said.

"Why not?"

"Because I don't think she would help us."

"You mean you don't want to ask her to help," she guessed shrewdly. "Don't you like her?"

He stood up suddenly and placed his tea-cup and saucer down on the Benares ware table.

"Frankly, I can't see what she has to do with the matter we were discussing. Will you or won't you design some more outfits? You could choose the colours for the tweeds and they could be specially woven."

"Yes, I will, Sandy, if that's what you would like, because I'm not happy unless I'm designing clothes, but it doesn't matter what I do, it won't get you anywhere unless you have some good publicity in the more expensive magazines, as your mother suggested. And Sarah Popham might be able to help you to get that."

He turned his back on her and walked over to the sideboard where he picked up one of the many Christmas cards still displayed there. Lisa watched him sensing the emotional turmoil her mention of Sarah had roused.

"At this very moment I expect she's meeting Fraser Lamont in London," she said carelessly.

He replaced the card carefully in the position he had found it and turned to face her.

"How do you know?" he asked.

"I heard him making the arrangement with her one day when I was in his office."

"What were you doing there?" he queried with a lilt of surprise in his voice.

"Oh, I rescued his boy from a fight and took him home."

"And gave him a piece of your mind for neglecting his child," he suggested with a smile.

It was Lisa's turn to be surprised.

"How do you know?" she challenged back.

"I met Fraser just before he left for London. He has a stand at the Boat Show and he's had to take Johnnie with him. The day of the fight Mrs. Dobie gave notice because Johnnie kicked her while she was trying to attend to his black eye, so there was no one to look after him while Fraser went away."

"But what will a child like that do at the Show?"

"Stay on the stand, I expect, with Fraser, or wander around getting into mischief. Who knows? Maybe Sarah will try her hand at looking after him."

"I would have looked after him here and he could have continued to go to school when it starts next week," asserted Lisa, temporarily forgetting that Fraser had ordered her to stay away from his child.

Sandy chuckled.

"Can you imagine your Aunt Maud's reaction when she found you giving shelter to the son of her arch-enemy?" he remarked.

"But surely there's someone in the village who would have taken him. Your mother doesn't seem to dislike Fraser as much as some others I've met."

"Mother would, but then she would have to contend with my father. And then there's Fraser's attitude to take into consideration. Since the episode with Marjorie Morrison he's been very wary about asking anyone in the village to mind Johnnie. Of course the best arrangement would be for him to marry again and provide the child with a stepmother."

"Sarah Popham, perhaps," she suggested, watching him closely. "Aren't you jealous when you think of them meeting tonight in London?"

"No. I don't begrudge Sarah any happiness if she can find it with Fraser or anyone else. She's had a very unhappy time lately," he replied rather stiffly.

"So you do love her," probed Lisa.

"I used to be in love with her," he said rather wistfully. "I asked her to marry me, but she wanted to go away to London to make her name as a model. Who was I to stand in her way? I had nothing to offer. She was fascinated by the jet-set way of life with which she came into contact and married Jack Popham . . . his third wife!"

"More fool she," observed Lisa. "Well, if you won't ask her to help you by using her contacts and influence I shall. The only problem is when and how can I meet her? Do you think she'll be back from London?"

"Yes. I should think she went only to be with her mother and father while they went to the Boat Show. She wouldn't want to stay at Creddon Hall by herself. She isn't really interested in boats."

Lisa's eyes narrowed thoughtfully as she tried to see into the future.

"But she might become interested if she thought that was the only way of holding a man who has attracted her," she murmured.

The New Year opened quietly. The weather was mild and by the middle of January Aunt Maud had recovered sufficiently to come downstairs for the afternoons. Her mind as needle-sharp as ever, she sat at the window of the sitting room and watched the waters of the kyle change colour as the sky above changed also.

"They don't seem to be building anything yet down there near the shore," she said one afternoon when Lisa came in from her walk. "Perhaps he hasn't been able to get permission after all. Or perhaps he's run out of money."

"Oh, I shouldn't think so. Johnnie was telling me yesterday that his father received many orders for fibre glass yachts at the Boat Show," replied Lisa.

"You've been seeing a lot of that child recently," grunted Aunt Maud.

"Yes, I meet him on his way home from school when I'm out with the dogs," said Lisa coolly.

Aunt Maud gave her an underbrowed glance which expressed plainly her disapproval.

"Does his father approve?" she asked.

"He doesn't know. At least I don't think Johnnie has told him."

"And I can tell you why. He knows his father wouldn't approve. I don't approve either. Do you realise, Lisa, you're encouraging that child to practise deceit towards his parent?"

49

"I can't see why anyone should disapprove of me talking to him. He's a very intelligent and sensitive boy, and he doesn't get enough attention. Actually I was thinking of bringing him here one day to meet you. I think you'd enjoy his company. And it would do him good to meet you and find out that you're not the old witch he thinks you are."

Aunt Maud stared at her haughtily for a moment, undecided whether to be offended or not. Then she broke into one of her delighted laughs.

"Is that what he thinks I am?"

"Yes, he thought I was a witch when we met on the ferry boat coming here because I was wearing a cloak. But he thinks you're the sort of witch who has a cauldron which you stir when you want to cast spells, and at the moment he believes you've cast a spell over George Morrison so that he won't sell The Moorings to a certain person."

"Whatever would make him think that?" demanded Aunt Maud sharply.

"He overheard his father say to George when they met one day, 'So the old witch has you in her power too, has she?' Aunty, have you been threatening George in some way?"

"I? Threaten?" exclaimed Aunt Maud. "I'd never do such a thing! I merely suggested to George that if he dared to sell The Moorings to Lamont I'd let the whole village know that his daughter was a liar as well as a thief."

"A thief? Are you sure?"

"Of course I'm sure. She came to work for me once. I was sorry for the lass. Then I began to miss little things – small items of jewellery, little ornaments, then some money. I had George over and told him what I suspected and agreed to keep quiet about it because he said he would deal with her. She denied everything."

"Then if you know she told lies you don't believe what she said about Fraser Lamont."

"No, I didn't believe it. Whatever else I might think about the man I couldn't believe he was lecherous. He's too open and direct in his manner for that."

Lisa thought of blue-black eyes which regarded her directly and honestly, of a square-jawed, fresh-complexioned face and of the pride expressed in the set of straight shoulders and the hard line of a well-shaped mouth. As Sandy had said, once she had met Fraser she could not believe the story told by Marjorie Morrison either, but she was pleased to hear her aunt express her disbelief too.

"Well, I must say I didn't realise my only aunt was a blackmailer," she teased, referring to Aunt Maud's hold over George Morrison.

"I've no objections to him selling to anyone else," said Maud huffily. Then changing the subject adroitly, she asked, "Have you heard from your father yet?"

"Yes. He says he hopes to get some leave soon because he's due for a change of commission, but he doesn't say when."

"If I know anything about Frank Smith he'll let you know the day before he is due to arrive and expect you to drop everything and run to meet him," remarked Aunt Maud. She sighed suddenly and gazed out at the waning sunlight. "Yes, I think I'd like to meet that little boy. His paternal grandmother died some time ago, poor soul, and the other one, whoever she is, doesn't seem to have much interest in him. Bring him tomorrow."

Next afternoon when they reached the end of the narrow lane leading to Breck House Johnnie surprised Lisa by asking if he could come with her to see the old witch.

"Yes, you can. As a matter of fact she wants to meet you," she replied.

"Really?"

"Really. And if she likes you she might ask you again and show you some of her treasures."

"What sort of treasures?"

"Interesting things from places like China, India and Japan."

"Has she any puzzles or games?"

"I believe she has."

"Then I'll come."

"You won't be able to stay for long, Johnnie," Lisa warned. "She's an old lady and she's been very ill, so she gets tired easily. Also I expect your housekeeper will be waiting for you."

"We're managing without one," he said, with that odd little grown-up air he sometimes assumed.

"Then who is doing the cleaning and the cooking?"

"Daddy. He's a good cook, better than Mrs. Dobie, and he lets me help him. But he isn't very good at cleaning and there's a lot of dust. Sarah came to see us the other day, but she only eats, she doesn't cook. She says she can't. Don't you think that's silly, Lisa? A lady who can't cook? She wouldn't be much good as a mother. All mothers cook and clean."

Out of the mouth of a seven-year-old boy, thought Lisa with a private grin. Here was the traditional male outlook that women were made to cook and clean and look after children. Yet from all accounts he had not learned it from his father, who considered himself capable of doing all those things without any assistance from a woman.

Johnnie's first visit to Breck House went off without a hitch. Both he and Aunt Maud were on their best behaviour. The visit was repeated the next day, then there was a pause because of the week-end, but on the following Monday he came again and continued to come every schoolday after that. Sometimes he talked to Aunt Maud as she rummaged through her boxes of "treasure" or played simple card games with her. When she was tired he stayed in the kitchen with Lisa, who showed him how to use poster paints and a paintbrush, having discovered he liked nothing better than to create fantastic pictures.

Whether he told his father what he was doing during the hour after school Lisa did not ask as she did not want to spoil the pleasure he seemed to derive from visiting her and her aunt.

One afternoon towards the end of January when the days were beginning to lengthen Johnnie and Lisa were so absorbed that they forgot the time and realised with a shock that it was almost half-past five, long past the time when Johnnie usually left. Lisa hurried him out of the house and down the brae and went with him into the boatyard thinking that if Fraser was angry she could do the explaining and spare the boy a little of his father's wrath.

As they approached the steps of the white house a woman got out of a car which was parked nearby, and came towards them. She was of medium height, slim and elegantly dressed, and had long curling honey-coloured hair.

"So there you are, Johnnie," she said in a high-pitched, slightly shrill voice. "Your father has gone to look for you."

"I've been at Lisa's house and Aunt Maud gave me this," said Johnnie, holding out a model of an elephant carved in ebony complete with ivory tusks.

The woman ignored both his answer and the elephant and stared curiously at Lisa.

"Are you Lisa Smith?" she asked, her speedwell blue eyes taking in every detail of Lisa's clothing.

"Yes, I am. You're Sarah Popham, the model, aren't you?"

"I'd have been mortified if you hadn't recognised me," laughed the other. "Mrs. Lewis was talking about you to me only this afternoon. She says you design clothes. I haven't time to talk about this now . . . I was just going to drive home when you appeared with Johnnie, but I'd like you to design something for me to be made in one of the Ardmont tweeds. Could you come to lunch next Friday?"

"Yes, I think so," agreed Lisa, her quick mind leaping ahead, thinking how she could use this surprising turn of events to advantage, not only for herself, but also for Sandy.

"Fraser is coming then to talk to Daddy about the yacht he's bought, so perhaps he could bring you over," said Sarah. She looked past Lisa towards the entrance to the yard. "Here he is now, so you can make arrangements with him."

Lisa turned to glance at the approaching man while Johnnie dashed up the steps of the house, flung open the front door and disappeared.

"Johnnie was quite safe after all, Fraser," said Sarah

sweetly. "He was with Lisa and her aunt."

Fraser ignored her and walked straight up to Lisa. She could see by the fading light that anxiety had sharpened the angles of his face and had drawn new lines about his mouth.

"I thought I told you to stay away from Johnnie," he said sharply to her.

He spoke as if Sarah was not there, as if there were only the two of them standing in the shaft of yellow light which slanted through the swiftly falling dusk from the open doorway.

Lisa's chin came up and her eyelids dropped haughtily as she reacted to the reprimand in his voice.

"He asked me if I would take him to see the old witch one day. I couldn't refuse a request like that. He's been coming every day. They get along very well and it's good for both of them. Today we were so busy we forgot the time," she replied coolly.

Some of the tautness went out of his face and his mouth twitched humorously.

"The old witch," he repeated softly. "I'm afraid he learned that from me."

"Fraser," Sarah's voice was slightly pettish in tone as she resented being ignored, "I have to go now. Lisa is coming to lunch next Friday too. You could bring her, couldn't you? About twelve-thirty?"

Fraser slanted her a cold glance.

"Lisa has the use of her aunt's car, so she doesn't have to depend on me to drive her to Creddon Hall," he said, making no secret of the fact that he was not to be regarded as a chauffeur for anyone who wished to go to the Hall.

If she had any pride, real pride she would have walked away there and then, thought Lisa of herself. But she did not move.

Sarah shrugged.

"Oh well, have it your own way. If you want to come separately that's fine with me. Your aunt should be able to tell you how to get to the Hall Lisa. It isn't far, and by then I should have some tweed for Mrs. Lewis. Goodbye for now."

As she passed Fraser on the way to her car she glanced up at him rather coyly.

"I don't suppose it's any use asking you to walk to the car with me see me into it, and close the door for me?" she purred provocatively.

"No use at all," he answered with a grin.

"No one could ever accuse you of being a ladies' man, Fraser," Sarah grumbled with a return to her earlier petulance.

"And that's the way I like it," he returned equably. "Good night, Sarah."

With a petulant twitch of her shoulders she went off to her car and Lisa made a move to go. With a quick sidestep Fraser blocked the way.

"Don't think you're going to get away so easily," he murmured threateningly. "I've something to say to you, Red Smith."

As Sarah turned her car towards the entrance of the yard the shafts of light from the headlamps swept over them.

"Come into the house," ordered Fraser curtly.

"Do you think that would be wise?" asked Lisa with a touch of mockery. "If anyone sees me going in with you there's no knowing what they'll think. Remember the village tittle-tattle?"

Sarah seemed to be having some difficulty with her car because it was still there, its engine idling.

"If you don't come in and explain what's been going on after school for the last week or so, Johnnie will probably get a belting for lying," said Fraser quietly.

"Oh no, you wouldn't," objected Lisa anxiously. The car was now moving forward slowly.

"Wouldn't I?" he scoffed. "You forget he's my child and I'm responsible for disciplining him. He knows he should come straight home after the school bus has dropped him in the village and that he gets punished if he doesn't obey my instructions. This time I've a feeling he isn't wholly to blame for being disobedient. His story is that he's been staying behind to help the teacher and coming on the usual bus. But

55

since he has no money for his fare that's barely credible, and now seeing you here with him this evening makes me think you're behind all this. Well, are you coming in or not?"

"I'll come," she said resignedly, noting that Sarah's car had at last reached the entrance of the yard and was turning out on to the main shore road.

"But there are other ways of punishing a child without resorting to physical violence," she added.

"I know. I find them quite ineffectual, and my patience is wearing a little thin," he grated, closing the front door behind them. Then raising his voice he called out, "You can come out of hiding now, Johnnie, and do a little explaining!"

Taking off his jacket, he flung it over a chair in the hallway and said abruptly,

"Come into the kitchen. I have to get a meal ready, and while I'm doing that you can tell me why you decided to ignore my request to leave Johnnie alone and why you've been enticing him up to Breck House."

"I haven't enticed him," she denied hotly, sitting down on a kitchen chair and watching him take dishes and cooking utensils out of cupboards and drawers, then move across to the table to twitch the cloth straight, brush off the crumbs made by another meal and begin to set it with cutlery. The room was far better than she had imagined. It was bright and clean and although not exactly tidy there were no dirty dishes about.

"I told you he asked if he could come and see Aunt Maud," she said, continuing her defence.

The glance he gave her was sceptical as he left the table and went over to the refrigerator, opened it and took out some eggs which he proceeded to break into a mixing bowl.

"He wouldn't have asked if he hadn't been seeing you regularly and become used to you. You see, I know him rather better than you do. He doesn't ask favours of strangers," he said, and began to whisk the eggs.

"That's one way in which he's like you," observed Lisa calmly, noticing how deft and efficient were his movements. He had obviously had plenty of experience in whisking eggs.

"What makes you think that?" he asked, giving her a sharp underbrowed glance.

"You didn't have to take him to the Boat Show with you. I would have looked after him for you, but you didn't ask me because you didn't know me well enough," she replied.

He stopped beating the eggs and turned to the cooker to switch on a hot plate.

"Whereas you're so clever you can assess a person's character before you've even met him," he said with a touch of sarcasm. "Yes, I am cautious about strangers, especially where Johnnie is concerned. I have reason to be. Now what do you hope to gain by encouraging him?"

"Oh, I suppose it's because you do everything out of self-interest that you think everyone must do the same," retorted Lisa angrily. "I don't hope to gain anything. I met Johnnie on the boat coming over here and I felt concerned about him because he had no mother and apparently you didn't care a hang what happened to him."

He had reached into a cupboard for a heavy frying pan and before turning to place it on the cooker he gave her another sceptical glance which did nothing to soothe her anger.

"I don't expect you to understand for one minute," she seethed, "but what I'm telling you is the truth. I thought I could help him by meeting him and talking to him after school and when I discovered there was no one here in the house for him to come home to ... not even Mrs. Dobie ... I thought it would do no harm to take him up to see Aunt Maud as he asked. She said herself he seemed to have no grandmother so that perhaps she could provide that lack in his life."

He had his back to her now and was heating butter in the frying pan. All she could see was the straight proud set of his shoulders and the way his thick brown hair had a tendency to curl at the nape of his neck. When eventually he turned back to the bowl of eggs she noticed that his mouth was set in that hard straight line, giving nothing away, and that his eyes were hidden as he looked down at the bowl rather than at her. He gave a final whisk to the eggs, picked up the bowl and turned back to the cooker, having said nothing. He poured the contents of the bowl into the pan and stood and watched the result, apparently far more interested in his cooking than in anything she had to say in her own defence.

From the hallway came the sound of a stair creaking as someone stepped upon it. Lisa guessed that Johnnie was creeping slowly down on his way to make an explanation.

"Have I answered your question?" she asked Fraser.

He did not seem to hear her because he did not turn round, nor did he answer, being too engrossed in his cooking.

"Mr. Lamont," she persisted, because it was most important for some reason that she should make him understand that her interest in Johnnie was purely altruistic, "have I answered your question? Do you understand now why I ignored your request to stay away from Johnnie?"

This time he heard her or, at least, he acknowledged that she had spoken, because he half-turned and gave her a narrowed sidelong glance.

"Yes, you've answered it, in a way, but I'm not sure I understand your motives yet. I wouldn't like him to develop too much of a liking for you, because he'll be upset when you go away."

"But I'm not going away. I'm going to stay and look after Aunt Maud and there's a possibility that I might go to work for Sandy Lewis."

At that point Johnnie burst suddenly into the room. He was still in his duffle coat and he was clutching his ebony elephant in his hand. He went straight up to Fraser and held up the elephant for him to see.

"Miss Roy gave me this," he said breathlessly, hoping to divert his father's anger by drawing his attention to the gift. "She isn't an old witch, like you said, she's just an old lady. You . . . you're not cross with Lisa and me any more, are you?"

Fraser crossed his arms over his chest, leaned against the sink unit and looked down at the child. His mouth twitched a little with amusement, but he put on a pretence of frowning severely.

"Yes, I am. But not as cross as I was. Next time you decide to go visiting Miss Roy on the way home from school it would be better if you told me instead of making up stories about staying behind at school to help the teacher and then I'm not so likely to rush off and make a fool of myself looking all over the village for you. You know the rule, Johnnie. You come straight home from school and report to me when I'm here before you do anything else."

Johnnie's long eyelashes fluttered down over his eyes and his mouth quivered.

"Yes, Daddy," he muttered. Then with a quick change of mood he looked up again and said impulsively, "Can Lisa stay to supper?"

"Would you like her to do that?"

Johnnie nodded his head vigorously, his eyes shining hopefully.

"She's a very good cook," he said. "I had some of her scones this afternoon."

"You're lucky," remarked Fraser with a touch of dryness in his voice. "Next time you have tea out you might think of me and hide some of those scones in your pockets. I haven't had a decent home-made scone for years." He glanced across at Lisa and added, "Will you stay and share our supper?"

She had a great longing to stay, to help prepare the meal and to clear away the dishes afterwards and then to put Johnnie to bed and possibly read a bedtime story to him. It was a most extraordinary desire and it frightened her.

She stood up quickly.

"Thank you for the invitation," she stammered, with less than her usual poise. "But I think it would be wiser if I didn't stay." Then she saw mockery gleam in Fraser's dark eyes and she continued hurriedly, "Aunt Maud is alone and she must be wondering where I am."

"Then of course it wouldn't be wise for you to stay," he agreed blandly, ignoring Johnnie's loud protest, and Lisa had the impression that he was relieved by her refusal and immediately felt a most unusual resentment that he should accept it so easily.

"Then can I go to Breck House again tomorrow after school?" persisted Johnnie. "Miss Roy said she'd teach me how to play dominoes. Please, Daddy."

"No." The refusal was uncompromising.

"Why?" wailed Johnnie.

"Miss Roy doesn't like me much and I wouldn't want you to be a nuisance to her."

"He isn't a nuisance," began Lisa impulsively.

"I still don't want him to go to Breck House," was the icy reply, accompanied by a supercilious glance which told her quite clearly that Fraser resented her interference.

Tilting her chin, she moved towards the door.

"Watch the omelette, Johnnie, please," ordered Fraser, crossing the room to Lisa's side. "I'll see Miss Smith to the front door."

"Oh, don't bother," she said airily. "I know you don't like to be regarded as a ladies' man."

He raised an eyebrow at her.

"All right, be independent. See yourself out," he said softly. "But don't blame me if you fall down the steps in the dark. Good night, Red Smith."

As soon as she closed the front door behind her she realised what he had meant. The thick door cut off all the light from the hallway and it was a while before her eyes became accustomed to the darkness. Although she went carefully she miscounted the steps, found there was one more than she had thought on which she tripped, lost her balance and fell to her knees.

"Talk about pride coming before a fall," she muttered to herself. "That should teach you to refuse to be escorted to the front door in the future, Lisa Smith!"

She got to her feet and was glad to find that the ankle which had turned under her would take her full weight. It would have been very humiliating if she had been forced to ask Fraser for help.

How right Sarah had been when she had said no one could accuse him of being a ladies' man. He made no concessions to the so-called weaker sex. Lisa guessed that he always spoke to a woman as he would speak to a man, using no cajolery or flattery to soften his approach, and if the woman did not like it she could lump it. When she thought about it that was how she had always wanted to be treated, as an equal, no holds barred.

The wind moaned eerily and a few flakes of snow drifted into her face brushing her skin like icy feathers. She pulled her hat down more firmly and buried her face in her scarf as she hurried up the brae to Breck House, wondering why Fraser had been so adamant in his refusal to allow Johnnie to go again to visit Aunt Maud. He had said it was because he did not want the child to be a nuisance to someone who did not like himself, which meant his pride was stepping in there, but she had a suspicion that there was another reason and that it was closely connected with herself.

Next morning she went to the mill to tell Sandy that she had at last met Sarah.

"We met by accident at the boatyard. She's invited me to lunch next Friday and she wants me to design some clothes for her, to be made from Ardmont tweed, so I might be able to do a deal with her, and persuade her to model the clothes for advertising purposes."

"I hope you can," said Sandy. "Come up to the farmhouse and see the tweed which Mother is weaving for you. It's going to be superb."

So once again Lisa spent an enthralling morning admiring Mrs. Lewis's handiwork which included a new tweed for which she herself had chosen the colours, the delicate mauves and pinks of a winter sunset as seen reflected in the water of the kyle.

It was as she was leaving that she noticed the two sheepskins, stretched on wooden frames for curing, lying in a corner of the room. Touching the white curly wool, she asked Sandy who they belonged to.

"They're Sheila's, my brother Hugh's wife. She had a fancy for a sheepskin jacket and I said I'd get one made for her. Curing and tanning them is as far as I've got with them."

"I could dye them and make a jacket for her," offered Lisa.

"You could?" he looked surprised. They stared at each other across the frame as the same thought struck both of them. "Lisa, do you think you could design sheepskin jackets as well as tweed clothing?"

"I could dye the skin one of the colours used in a tweed and match them in an outfit," she replied excitedly. "Do you think Sheila would let me have these skins to experiment with?"

"I know she would. But what are you going to use for dye?"

"I'm going to use green ink," announced Lisa.

Exhilarated by her morning, she drove back to Breck House in high spirits. As Sandy had once said it did seem as if her quarrel with Richard Hatton had been fortuitous. Here in Ardmont she felt at home in a way she had never felt in Manchester. She guessed that the feeling was closely associated with the fact that she was no longer tied to Richard's routine. Here she was, free at last to realise her potential as a fashion designer and Sandy's undisguised enthusiasm for her designs had acted as a spur to her inventiveness. Yes, she thought, she could be very happy living here in Ardmont, designing for Ardmont Tweeds Ltd. occasionally and for other companies later when her designing ability became known.

Full of this idea, she went straight into the sitting room when she reached Breck House to tell Aunt Maud. She found her sitting in her usual high-backed, wing chair staring out of the window. It was not until she was close to her that she saw that the old lady was shaking with rage.

"Why, Aunty, whatever is the matter?" she asked, anxiously afraid that such anger might bring on another heart attack.

"Matter? That's the matter." Aunt Maud raised her stick and pointed with it. On the land beyond the shore road adjacent to the water a group of men were unloading from a lorry the girders and frames necessary for building a shed. "Have you no eyes in your head, lass?" barked Aunt Maud. "Didn't you see them as you drove along the road?"

"No. I was thinking of something else. Mr. Lamont must have received permission to build after all."

"Aye, he must. As soon as I saw them I rang up. He wasn't there. Jean Bridie told me he'd had to go into Kilbride to the school about that precious brat of his. So I told her that as soon as he came back I wanted to see him up here, and that he was to bring me proof that he has permission. He's taking his time to come, though. I suppose he thinks he can ignore me now that he's got his own way."

"Maybe he has other things to do," said Lisa soothingly.

"Are you sticking up for him?" demanded Aunt Maud.

"No, but I don't think he'll ignore you. He isn't afraid of you."

"That's the trouble," grunted Aunt Maud grudgingly.

It was almost three-thirty when the doorbell rang. Lisa answered its summons. Fraser looked much the same as when she had seen him the previous night. He was wearing the same sweater and pants, but instead of sea-boots and a wind-cheater he was wearing polished brogues and a tweed jacket. In one hand he held a buff envelope, and he did not reply to her greeting as he stepped into the hallway but went on to the sitting room as if sure of his way. She hurried after him and was surprised to hear him greet Aunt Maud quite pleasantly, as if they were old friends instead of enemies.

"Good afternoon, Miss Roy. How are you today?"

"I've felt better, Fraser Lamont. Looking out of this window this morning did not improve my state of health. So you got your own way after all."

By way of answer he held out the envelope to her. She snatched it from him, pulled out the letter it contained, read it, then made a frustrated exclamation as she pushed it back into the envelope and handed it back to him.

"I can't understand those County people. One minute

they're saying they don't want anyone to build an eyesore to spoil the countryside and the next they're giving permission to someone to erect ugly sheds on common land."

"The shed that will be built there will be no worse than Ardmont Mill which sticks up at the back of the village like a sore thumb, and that land isn't common land. It has belonged to Lamonts for over a hundred years, as I was able to prove to the County Council as I still have the original deeds of ownership showing the boundaries."

"Then why didn't your grandfather or your father build on it?" demanded Aunt Maud.

"Because they didn't need to. They had no wish to expand. My grandfather was able to support his family and keep the business going by turning out about seven yachts a year. My father as you know failed miserably. I don't intend to follow in his footsteps," said Fraser grimly. "These days the yachting business is much more competitive and to survive you have to mass-produce boats as well as build the traditional wooden ones. I have many orders for fibre glass boats this year and I need that shed. Now if you'd been sensible instead of sentimental you'd have sold me your property and then you wouldn't be sitting here complaining about your view being spoilt, although when your hedge grows up in the summer you'll hardly see the shed."

All the time he was speaking Aunt Maud did her best to interrupt him, but he ignored her attempts by raising his voice slightly above hers until he had finished what he wanted to say. Then he turned to her and said with a cheeky grin,

"Your turn now."

"If I'm sentimental you're as hard as nails, and rude too, not letting an old woman speak!" she spluttered.

"I was always taught that it's rude to interrupt when someone is speaking," he replied coolly. "You are sentimental, you know, keeping an old house like this which is damp and riddled with woodworm, hanging on to a big garden which you can't afford to have tended, all because of 'false pride in blood and place'."

"Humph, quote Tennyson at me, would you? False pride, indeed, and I suppose you think you have none?" retorted Aunt Maud.

"If you'd sold it to me in the autumn when I offered you could have gone to live in a pleasant flat in Largs or Rothesay, and then perhaps you wouldn't have been so ill."

"I've told you before, I intend to hand this house on to another Roy," muttered Aunt Maud. "And you needn't think you're going to squeeze me out by buying The Moorings. I've told George Morrison not to sell to you."

"Well, you can take the pressure off him now," returned Fraser, who did not seem at all surprised by her admission. "I've changed my mind. Now that I have this," he held up the envelope, "I'm not so desperate and I can afford to bide my time. I hope you're satisfied now that what I'm doing down there is all legal and above board."

"Yes," admitted Aunt Maud grudgingly. "But that doesn't mean to say I'm pleased, so you can tell that brat of yours he needn't bother to come up here again. The sight of him reminds me too much of you and you remind me too much of your grandfather, and when I think of what both of you have done in your time to me. . . ." She paused, breathing heavily, and Lisa moved close to her, anxiously.

"It wasn't my idea that Johnnie should come here anyway," said Fraser softly. "Goodbye, Miss Roy. If you should change your mind and decide you'd like to sell, just let me know."

Without a glance at Lisa he walked out of the room. Her conscience pricking her about Johnnie, she went after him catching up with him as he opened the door.

"I'm sorry about what Aunt Maud said about not wanting to see Johnnie again," she said. "I hope he isn't too upset about not coming."

He shrugged his shoulders carelessly.

"He'll get over it," he said curtly.

"Like you did when your mother sold up and moved away from here and when your wife died, I suppose," she snapped angrily, annoyed by his hardness.

She could tell by the sudden blaze in his eyes that he was offended by her personal remarks, but he made no effort to retaliate.

"There's nothing to stop me from seeing Johnnie on his way home from school. Neither Aunt Maud nor you can stop that," she continued, goaded by his silence.

"You won't see him today," he returned coldly. "He's in hospital at Inverey."

"Why, what's happened to him?" she whispered, fear curling round her heart.

"He had an accident in the school playground. He has concussion." He recited this information without showing a flicker of emotion.

"Oh, I'm sorry," said Lisa helplessly. She wanted to offer comfort and sympathy, but his attitude gave her no encouragement. She wanted also to rush off to the hospital to see Johnnie. But she had no rights where he was concerned, none at all. Yet she could not help trying.

"I'll go and see him," she announced.

"No." His refusal came out like a pistol shot.

"Why not? Maybe I can help him?"

He gave her one of those narrowed sceptical glances which made her blood start to simmer.

"If you want to help you'll stay away from Johnnie," he said cryptically, and went through the door, closing it behind him sharply, leaving her gaping at the bunches of grapes which patterned on the Victorian glass panel of the door.

CHAPTER IV

WITH all the easily roused emotionalism of the old and the ill Aunt Maud was very upset when Lisa told her about Johnnie's accident and for the rest of the afternoon she bemoaned the fact that she had called the child a brat and had said he wouldn't be welcome at Breck House any more.

"I wouldn't have said it if I'd known. I only said it because I wanted to annoy his father in some way. Fraser is so hard that it's difficult to find weapons with which to hurt him. I thought perhaps the bairn was his weak spot and that if I hurt the child I'd hurt the man. Do you understand, Lisa?"

Lisa nodded, thinking of her own feeble attempts to annoy Fraser. Perhaps it was true after all; he was hard all the way through and nothing could touch his heart.

"You must ring up and enquire about the bairn every day," said Aunt Maud. "Find out if we can send something to him to show that we remember him."

"Yes, I'll do that," agreed Lisa, "Aunty, what do you think he meant when he said he could afford to bide his time?"

"I think he meant that he can afford to wait now until he can get what he wants, and we know that he wants Breck House. Promise you won't let him have it when I've gone, Lisa."

"Couldn't you make some legal arrangement covering that?" asked Lisa. "I'm sure Murdo Menzies could write something into your will. I would feel much happier and safer if you did that."

"That's a good idea. I'll get Murdo to come and see me." She sighed wearily. "Still, I'd like to know what yon rascal has up his sleeve. Do you think you could find out?"

"I'll try, but I can't promise I'll find out anything. Mr. Lamont isn't exactly well disposed towards me for some reason, so he isn't likely to tell me any of his plans for the future.

But sometimes he talks to Sandy, so maybe I can learn something from him," replied Lisa comfortingly.

As Aunt Maud had instructed her she rang the boatyard every day for news of Johnnie. Every time Jean Bridie provided the information in a cool impersonal voice. Lisa often wondered whether the primly-spoken woman was briefed by Fraser about what she should or should not say about the child's condition, because she supplied only the barest and briefest answers to Lisa's persistent and concerned queries.

"Yes, he had a fairly good night and is as well as can be expected," was her usual answer, which always had the effect of setting Lisa's teeth on edge.

One morning, irritated by the treatment she was receiving and convinced that Fraser was behind it, she asked Jean Bridie whether it would be possible for her to go to the hospital to visit Johnnie as she had a gift for him. Although pushed slightly off balance by the unexpected request, Jean had an answer.

"Ach, no, miss, that would never do. Ye see, the doctors says rest is the only cure and the excitement caused by visitors will do the bairn no good at all. Even Mr. Lamont isn't visiting him."

Frustrated by Jean's sparsely worded answers and horrified by what she considered to be inhuman behaviour on the part of Fraser in not visiting his child, Lisa rang the hospital immediately and asked for information about Johnnie, only to be told coolly that since she was not a relative of his they could not divulge any information to her about him.

Thoroughly roused by now, Lisa decided to drive over to Inverey, the county town twenty miles distant from Ardmont where the hospital was situated. Once she was there surely they could not refuse to tell her how he was, or at least to let her leave some fruit for him?

However, she was forced to change her mind about going as the result of a rather strange telephone conversation with Sarah Popham which left her shaken and bewildered.

Sarah rang up to remind her of the luncheon party which

would be taking place at Creddon Hall on the next day.

"I hope you haven't forgotten about it?" said the model in her shrill voice.

"No, I haven't. I've plenty to show you and to tell you," said Lisa warmly, thinking of the different outfits she had drawn for Sarah to appraise and also of the success she had had with dyeing the sheepskins.

"Oh, good. I'm so bored I could scream. I talked to Fraser earlier this week and he assured me he's still coming. It will be a change to have some stimulating company."

"Did he tell you about Johnnie?" asked Lisa.

"No. He didn't say anything about him and I make sure I never show an interest in the child because I know Fraser doesn't like it."

A strange chill swept over Lisa. She felt she was on the brink of learning something she would prefer not to know.

"Doesn't he? Why not?" she asked through stiff lips.

"Because he's tired of being pestered by women, some of whom he's employed as housekeepers, and who have fancied themselves as Johnnie's stepmother. They used the child to approach the father, if you get what I mean."

"How embarrassing for him," croaked Lisa, whose throat was suddenly dry.

"Yes, isn't it? But it's to be expected when you think how attractive he is. For myself I'd just loathe it if he thought like that about me, so I've decided never to ask about Johnnie or to show an interest in him, not that I need to use that form of aproach with any man," said Sarah with a smugness of attitude, which Lisa found totally out of tune with her own feelings on the subject. "Now tell me what's happened to Johnnie."

Subduing a strong inclination to bang the telephone receiver down and cut the conversation short, Lisa swallowed and answered as evenly as she could.

"He had an accident and he's in hospital. Concussion."

"Oh, dear! How frightful, and how terribly inconvenient for Fraser having to go and visit him. He's so very busy at the

69

yard just now. But then I expect you've been doing the visiting for him. You're so very fond of Johnnie, aren't you?"

The saccharine quality of Sarah's voice only emphasised the taunt implicit in her words. Lisa had no doubt about how Sarah Popham regarded her friendship with Johnnie.

"Yes, I am fond of Johnnie," she replied as coolly as she could. "I expect Fraser will tell you about the accident when we come to lunch tomorrow."

"Perhaps. But I wouldn't count on it. He and I have much more interesting subjects to discuss," replied Sarah with a coy little giggle. " 'Bye for now."

Lisa did not bang the receiver down. She laid it gently and carefully in its cradle and stood for a minute in the dimness of the hall breathing hard in order to control the sudden surge of rage which shook her.

So that was how she appeared to Fraser Lamont – as a pestering woman who was using his child to ingratiate herself with him. The conceit of the man. The egotistical conceit! And Sarah Popham saw her in the same light. Probably they had discussed her and had laughed about her.

The injustice of it all made her blood boil again and it took all her self-control to stop herself from marching out into the cold windy night, down to the white house at the back of the boatyard to tell Fraser Lamont in no uncertain terms what she thought of him. Above all she wanted to make it quite clear to him that marriage with a man who had already been married and who had a child, or with any other man was not in her plans for her future at all. And even if it had been she would never have stooped to using his child as a means of ensnaring him. She did not regard men as prey to be snared. Marriage was the culmination of love, and love could only exist where there was respect and equality.

Eventually she simmered down and went back to the kitchen, where she was dyeing the sheepskins with green ink. As she had expected the leather being porous readily absorbed anything liquid and the ink had produced a soft sage green reminiscent of the fields during the winter time. When she turned the white wool of the outside of the skin back against the green she was pleased with the contrast and began immediately to sketch a full-length coat with a close-fitting bodice and slightly flared skirt in which the white wool showed in two bands down the front fastening.

While she sketched her mind went back to her recent conversation with Sarah. Now that she was calmer she could see that it shed new light on Fraser's attitude to herself, and she began to understand his caution and his warning to her to stay away from Johnnie. He had been protecting himself, but not knowing her very well he had not realised that his adamant attitude had made her want to make friends with Johnnie all the more.

But she could not have him thinking she had had an ulterior motive in making friends with his child. She would have to prove to him in some way that she was not like that. She could not have him thinking badly about her.

Lisa's pencil slipped as she realised the direction her thoughts were taking. She stared at the black streak the pencil had made. Why should it matter to her what Fraser thought about her? She did not give a button for his opinion. Even so, it would be better if she did not go to visit Johnnie while he was in hospital and when he came home she would go very carefully indeed. She would not like to be responsible for increasing Mr. Fraser Lamont's conceit of himself.

The next day she took the dyed sheepskins and the drawings she had made to the mill to show Sandy. He was very interested in both and suggested that they went into the sheepskin coat business together.

"Or we can make it a family affair. The farm can supply the skins, you design the coats while I find someone to do the cutting and the sewing," he said.

"Yes, I've been wondering about that," replied Lisa. "We need someone to cut and sew the suits too. I can make my own clothes, but I'm not really a dressmaker or a tailor. Do you think Sheila would mind if I took these skins to show Sarah

Popham today? I've a feeling she might be interested in them."

"I'm sure Sheila won't mind."

"I wish you were coming with me."

"In some ways I wish I were too, and not for the reason you're thinking," he said with a smile. "Seriously, Lisa, you'll be far better at that sort of thing than I am. In fact if I could persuade you to become a partner in the firm I'll leave all the public relations to you as well as the designing."

"Fraser is going to lunch today too," she said.

"He'll be going to talk yachts to Harry Chisholm, I expect," he shrugged indifferently.

Lisa took a deep breath in order to control her impatience with him.

"I just don't understand you, Sandy Lewis! You say you're in love with Sarah, yet you make no attempt to approach her."

"I said I used to be in love with her," he corrected mildly. "Now I'm not so sure. She's obviously attracted to Fraser. He presents a challenge because he has no time for women. I only hope in her pursuit of him she doesn't get hurt again. He's pretty impregnable."

"I've noticed that. Have you any idea why?" she asked casually.

"No. I can only guess that he loved his wife so much that when she died he grew an extra hard shell to cover up his hurt, or his marriage was a mistake and turned him off women. He's never talked about it — in fact he's never mentioned his wife. We can only assume he was married because he came back with Johnnie."

"So you're not going to do anything about Sarah?"

"No. I tend to be a fatalist. Maybe she isn't for me. Maybe I'm going to find someone else with whom I can share my life, and possibly that someone is here in Ardmont, right under my nose."

Slightly disturbed by Sandy's final remark, Lisa left the mill and went to collect Mrs. Isabel Ramsay, a friend of Aunt Maud's who had agreed to stay at Breck House while Lisa was over at Creddon Hall. A widow, who lived alone on the other side of the village, Mrs. Ramsay was an active member of the Women's Rural Institute and an indefatigable churchgoer. She and Aunt Maud had very little in common except their schooling and their love of Ardmont, but these two common interests had been enough to keep them good companions in their old age.

The day, which had dawned fresh and clear, had clouded over by the time Lisa picked up Mrs. Ramsay and rain began to fall steadily, a grey curtain blotting out the island, stippling the sullen water of the kyle with big drops.

"Ye'll be needing to take care on the road to Creddon," warned Mrs. Ramsay. "The clouds come down low over the high parts and sometimes ye canna see where ye are going. And watch out for the bends. Keep well over to your left. Not that there'll be much on the road this time of the year."

Leaving in good time, Lisa did not hurry along the shore road as it wound up to the top of the cliffs beyond the boat-yard. It seemed to her that Aunt Maud's car, which was not in the first flush of youth, panted a little as if it disliked making such a strenuous effort and she was glad that the road flattened out for a few miles so that she was able to drive slowly and glance out occasionally at the northern arm of the kyle. Although it was blurred with rain she could just make out the small islands at the narrows. Immediately below the entrance to Loch Creddon opened up and soon the road began to rise again in a series of bends, some of which took the car right to the edge of the cliffs and some of which took it inland under a canopy of tall trees from whose branches raindrops dripped, drumming a tattoo on the roof of the car.

Up and up the road went so that the loch below was no longer a mass of moving water but appeared like a solid sheet of dull steel reflecting only the grey of the heavy clouds hovering above it.

As the car rounded what Lisa had hoped was the final steep bend and was faced with yet another incline its engine failed to pick up when she changed down to second gear for the long haul up. Slowly it chugged up, but as it approached

73

the top she could see steam issuing from under its bonnet. Fortunately there was a layby at the top and she was able to guide it off the road and to stop.

Having first discovered how to open the bonnet from a small booklet which she found in the glove compartment, Lisa stepped out into the clinging mist-like rain. The fact that steam had been coming out meant, she knew, that the engine was over-heated. She supposed that the climb had been too much for the car's age and condition. To go on would be to ruin the engine for ever. The only answer was to allow it to cool and possibly to find some water to put in it, all of which would make her late for lunch.

Vaguely she looked round to see if there was any water and then grinned when she saw it streaming down the rock beside her, but although she searched the inside and the boot of the car she could find no container in which she could carry water.

Then she heard the sound of a car's engine. It was coming from the direction of Ardmont. Relief seeped through her. Soon she was able to see the car as it took the slope much faster than hers had. It would not be long before it was near enough for her to signal. She stepped out and waved her long green scarf. The approaching car slowed down to a stop, a door opened and Fraser Lamont appeared.

"What's wrong?" he asked.

"Over-heated engine," she explained, thinking how attractive he looked in suit, shirt and tie with his rather unruly brown hair well tamed for once.

He gave her a slightly disparaging glance, strode over to the car lifted the top of the bonnet peered underneath, grunted, then closed it with a bang.

"Better leave it here to cool off. You can come with me," he said brusquely, nodding in the direction of his own car. "Get in."

"I've some things in the back of this car which I must take with me," she said hurriedly. She pulled forward the driver's seat of Aunt Maud's car and reached into the back seat for her drawings and the sheepskins.

As she backed out she banged her head on the top of the doorway, a blow which made her feel temporarily dizzy and also tipped her hat forward over her eyes. Intending to turn and thrust the things into Fraser's arms and tell him to put them in his car, she found that he was already sitting in the driver's seat of his car and apparently had no intention of helping her.

Tottering slightly, she walked over and tried to open the door of his car which was nearest to her. In the effort she dropped some of her drawings on the ground. Rage that he could sit there and let her struggle sizzled within her as she tried once more to pull the door open. This time she succeeded, and she thrust the sheepskins through the opening, saying between her teeth, "Here, put them in the back seat." Then she bent to pick up her mud-streaked drawings.

When she saw the state they were in she could have wept. She was tempted to hurl abuse at the man who sat waiting for her. But when she looked at him and met the slightly mocking gaze of his dark blue eyes she changed her mind quickly. If she were rude to him he was quite capable of driving off without her. So she placed the damaged drawings in his outstretched hand and said meekly,

"Do you think I should lock Aunt Maud's car?"

"Please yourself," he returned carelessly.

A great help he was! she thought rebelliously as she straightened her hat and locked the two doors. *Please yourself.* If that was the only answer he could give she must make sure never to ask him for advice again in future.

As soon as she was seated and the car door was closed he started the engine and drove off. The small high-powered car took the next incline with ease. Feeling damp after her brief stay out in the rain, Lisa sat taut and upright, looking straight before her, determined not to be first to break the silence. In fact she did not care if she never spoke to him again.

Her companion, however, had made no such resolution, for they had not gone far before he said easily,

"It was a pity you dropped your drawings. I hope they

aren't spoiled. They look interesting."

Although she longed to tell him that it was all his fault the drawings were damaged and that if he was a gentleman he would have helped her move the things from Aunt Maud's car to his she did not answer. She did not even look at him.

"Are they your reason for going to lunch with Sarah?" he asked politely.

"Yes." Brief to the point of rudeness.

"Are you a dress designer?" he persisted quietly

"Yes."

"That must be why you look so rakish."

She turned sharply, opened her mouth to object hotly to his description, then closed it when she saw the quirk of amusement at the corner of his mouth.

"I meant the word as a compliment, using it in its nautical sense," he explained smoothly. "A rakish ship has fine lines which show to advantage when it's well-maintained. Your style of clothing, which I presume you design yourself, flatters your height and your slender build."

She had forgotten that he was a designer too and as such would have an interest in good design in fields other than his own.

"Odd that we should have something in common, isn't it?" he remarked, as if he had read her thoughts, and she moved uneasily looking out at the dark dripping leaves of rhododendron bushes which lined this part of the road. The car was going downhill, now, swishing round bends as they approached the flatter land at the head of Loch Creddon.

"You're not usually so short of words," taunted Fraser. "Are you saving your conversation for the lunch table? Perhaps I should warn you that you'll not get a word in edgeways. Both Bunty and Harry Chisholm are great talkers. Another word of advice, if you're going to design anything for Sarah don't argue with her, just listen and then do what you think best. She's like her father. She knows a lot, has many ideas but is most impractical."

76

"Thank you for your advice, Mr. Lamont," she replied coolly. "I'll try to bear it in mind."

"I bet you won't," he retorted with a laugh. "You'll go your own way and be damned to me — which reminds me, you haven't asked me about Johnnie yet."

She stiffened in reaction.

"I don't intend to," she replied.

"Why not? Why the sudden loss of interest? Is it because you found it wasn't getting you anywhere?" he jeered.

It would be dangerous to hit him while he was driving, thought Lisa grimly, but that was the action she felt like taking. Instead she gritted her teeth and hissed between them,

"You're quite right. I decided the price I would have to pay to become his stepmother would be too great. I'd have to put up with you as a husband."

"Ouch!" he exclaimed mockingly. "You hit hard, Red Smith, but perhaps I deserved that one."

"It was nothing to what you'd have received if you hadn't been driving," she asserted. "You know very well I'm still interested in Johnnie. I've phoned Jean Bridie every morning since he went into hospital. But I won't have you thinking that I'm interested in him because I want a husband. Marriage is well down on my list of priorities for the future."

The silence which followed was not pleasant. Glancing at him out of the corner of her eye and noting the hard line of his mouth, Lisa felt once more that strange tremor of fear which she had experienced in his office the first time she had confronted him and wished it was possible to jump out of the car and run away from him.

The road was now bounded on either side by a low stone wall behind which stood tall trees. Twin gateposts appeared. Fraser swung the car between them and drove up a wide drive at the end of which stood a graceful grey building. He stopped the car in front of the entrance and Lisa prepared to get out.

Her hand was on the door handle when he spoke so pleasantly that she turned to look at him in surprise. He was leaning one elbow on the steering wheel and was watching her, his eyes narrowed, their expression unreadable.

"Thank you for speaking your mind," he said. "Now I have no doubt as to how you feel I must apologise for having been suspicious of your intentions. Shall we wipe the slate clean and start again?"

This tendering of the olive branch confused her so much that she could only answer stiltedly,

"If you wish."

"Then I'll begin by telling you that Johnnie is being discharged from hospital tomorrow. He's still having a few dizzy spells and he won't be able to go to school yet. But he can stay at home as long as he doesn't indulge in too much activity. It's going to be hard keeping him entertained and in one place."

"You could drop everything you're doing at the yard and look after him for once," she pointed out.

"What makes you think I'm not going to do that anyway?" he retorted. "Just because I don't go off the deep end and get all emotional every time he's hurt doesn't mean to say I don't know where my responsibilities to him lie."

"You didn't visit him when he was in hospital," she hissed. "I suppose you didn't think that came under the heading of responsibilities?"

"You know everything, don't you?" he observed sarcastically, "I didn't go to visit him because I was obeying the doctor's orders. There wasn't much point in going anyway because when I was able to go he was usually asleep." He broke off suddenly and then added with a rueful smile, "We're not doing very well with our clean slate, are we?"

He was right. Ever since she had agreed to wipe the slate clean she had snarled at him. If he had been guilty of suspecting her intentions she had been just as guilty of prejudice, of allowing other people's opinions of him to sway her judgement.

She looked up, ready to apologise, and met the blue blaze of his eyes as no longer narrowed in speculation their gaze lingered appraisingly on her face. He had not touched her and he did not touch her now, but for the first time she was aware of physical attraction flaring flamelike between them and understood at last why she felt that desperate urge to run away.

With a great effort she looked away from him down at her wrist watch.

"We're late," she muttered, and opening the door she scrambled out of the car as fast as she could.

Lisa was entranced by Creddon Hall, which was really a castle. Its clean uncluttered lines and quaint turrets expressed in pale grey stone appealed to her sense of design. Its setting too was perfect. Set on the banks of the river which flowed into Loch Creddon, backed by the smooth curves of Creddon Hill and surrounded by woods of spruce and larch, it was shown to advantage.

Inside simplicity combined with every modern convenience was the keynote. In the entrance hall bare stone walls were an excellent background for the crests and trophies which hung there. Stone walls were a predominant feature of the long dining room, pale contrast for the antique oak dining furniture and the collection of bronze shields which decorated the wall facing the long latticed windows.

Bunty Chisholm, Sarah's mother, was a plump pretty woman who came originally from the north of England, and it was not long before Lisa discovered that she was the driving force behind the restoration and preservation of the castle, which had once belonged to a sept of the Campbell clan and had at one time been a rallying point during various battles which had been waged in the area between the Campbells and other clans.

Harry Chisholm, on the other hand, was a small vigorous man from whom Sarah had inherited her speedwell blue eyes. He was, so Lisa learned from Bunty, the managing director of his family's company, which had been making pickles and preserves for many years.

Both were adept at putting their guests at ease, although Lisa noticed that the other guest, a young man who sported the latest in male hair styling and clothing, was nervous. His name was Peter Wright and he was a freelance photographer and close friend of Sarah.

Sarah, who was dressed in a long woollen dress which clung to her figure and which she had relieved with several gilt necklaces, was in an impish mood and during the meal Lisa wondered once or twice whether she would get any business done with the model that afternoon. Her main aim seemed to be to draw Fraser's attention to herself by flirting with Peter, but in that she was failing miserably, because Fraser was patently disinterested, being too absorbed in listening to his host talking about his new acquisition, a schooner he had bought in Portugal.

"It'll be the biggest hereabouts," Harry Chisholm was saying clearly. "Bigger than Ranald's. I'm tired of my brother-in-law sailing into the same anchorage and dropping his hook and seeing his topsides tower above mine. When I was in Portugal last year I saw this one and liked the look of it. Of course, it was still carrying cargoes. Wait until you see it. Beautiful ship."

"No good to windward," murmured Fraser. "You won't win many races in it in this part of the world."

"Wouldn't, eh? Well, I suppose you know what you're talking about. That boat you designed for Ranald is certainly a winner. Well, I've bought it now and I want you to do the alterations."

Lisa did not hear Fraser's reply because Mrs. Creddon leaned forward at this point to inform her that "Ranald" was Ranald Gow of the well-known whisky company and the husband of Harry's sister.

The meal came to an end and Harry took Fraser off to his study, Mrs. Creddon excused herself and Sarah slumped visibly. Looking considerably relieved, Peter Wright leaned back in his chair and lit a cigarette. Lisa came to the conclusion that if she did not take the initiative her visit to Creddon Hall would have been wasted.

"I've left my drawings in the car," she said, rising to her

feet. "Shall I bring them in here to show you?"

Sarah came out of her trance, blinked and asked Peter for a cigarette before she answered.

"No, we'll go to my sitting room upstairs. I keep all my stuff up there. When you've got your drawings come straight up the main stairway, turn right at the top and it's the second room along the passage."

They all left the room together and as Lisa went to the front entrance Sarah and Peter went upstairs. It was still raining outside and she ran back from the car in order to prevent the drawings and sheepskins from getting wet. She paused in the hall to glance through the drawings and placed the most badly marked ones at the bottom of the folder in which they were contained.

When she entered Sarah's sitting room Lisa had the distinct impression that she had interrupted an argument between Sarah and Peter, because as she appeared Peter left Sarah standing in the middle of the room and flung himself down in an armchair, a sulky expression on his face.

Sarah's face was pink and her blue eyes expressed hurt, but she smiled when she saw Lisa and came forward to take the folder of drawings from her. She showed immediate interest in the sheepskins and insisted on looking at the drawings of the coats Lisa had made. Since they were the mud-spattered ones Lisa drew them out with reluctance.

"I'm sorry they're so messy. I dropped them when I was taking them from my car and putting them in Fraser's," she explained.

"Oh, you came together after all," said Sarah sharply.

Quickly Lisa explained why Fraser had given her a lift.

"That was very clever of you," sighed Sarah, gazing down at the smudged drawings. "I wish I was as clever as you. Nothing I do seems to attract his attention. Yet he gives you lifts and invites you into his house. No, don't bother to deny it. I saw you go in that day we met at the boatyard. That's why I was so nasty to you on the phone the other evening."

"Do you want his attention?" asked Lisa curiously. Never

having wanted to deliberately attract a man's attention, she was rather revolted by Sarah's attitude.

"Of course she does," drawled Peter from the depths of the armchair. "She can't stand it when a man ignores her. She'll go to any lengths to attract him, even to the extent of flirting with me. Look, Sarah my love, Fraser Lamont might be every young girl's dream of a he-man, but I didn't come all the way from London to help you net him. I want to know if you're interested in modelling for me again."

"Oh, you know I am, Peter, but . . ." Sarah threw her hands wide in a dramatically helpless gesture.

Sensing that her moment to strike had come, Lisa snatched up the nearest drawing of a tweed outfit, grabbed one of the magazines she had noticed in a rack and went over to Peter.

"We . . . that is, Ardmont Tweeds Limited . . . are very interested in Sarah modelling for you if she can model clothes like this and appear in magazines like this," she said.

Peter took the drawing from her and studied it, then stared at the page of fashion photographs she showed him. As he returned them to her his dark eyes appraised her curiously.

"You'd make a good model yourself," he murmured. He sat forward, put out a long slim hand and turned her face sideways. "Good profile and interesting colouring. Why not model the clothes yourself? I'm more than willing to photograph you."

Aware suddenly of Sarah's dislike of his suggestion, Lisa moved away from him.

"Because I don't want to become a model and because we need good publicity fast," she replied calmly. "Sarah is well known both as a model and a personality. She has a way of making a rag look like a ball gown."

"Oh, do you think so, Lisa?" chirruped Sarah, enjoying the flattery. "How nice of you to say so. Would you really like me to model your designs?"

"Yes, I would . . . as long as they're made in Ardmont Tweed."

"To help Sandy Lewis," said Sarah, her blue eyes narrowing shrewdly. "Strange ... I never thought he would be the type to attract you. He had a *tendresse* for me once. Did you know?"

"Yes, he told me."

"Did he now? I wonder why? It would be rather fun to do something for him," drawled Sarah. Then suddenly she clapped her hands together and swung round on Peter. "Just think, Peter, you could use Creddon Hall for a background." She turned and rushed over to the table, scrabbled through the drawings and went back to him with one showing an elegant suit in gold and brown tweed. "Imagine me, in that, against the postern gate ... with daffodils blowing at my feet."

Peter studied the drawing and then looked up at her, his eyes crinkling at the corners in an amazingly affectionate smile.

"You're right," he agreed. "You'd look great, Sarah." His dark gaze passed on to Lisa, the expression changing from one of affection to one of dawning respect. "You certainly have a fresh approach to that old standby the good Scottish tweed. I wouldn't be surprised if the industry doesn't take a new lease of life when high society sees pictures of Sarah Popham in one of your creations."

"You'll help, then? Both of you?" asked Lisa breathlessly.

"Yes, for a fee, of course," replied Sarah. "I can hardly wait for those clothes to be made up. Who's going to cut and sew them? You'll have to be careful. Some people can make the most awful mess of a perfectly good design."

The rest of the afternoon passed quickly as the three of them planned which of the designs would look best made up. Lisa found that once Sarah had agreed to model the clothes she was sensible and had no hesitation in telling Lisa how to go about the business of publicity, so that by the time Fraser sent word to say that he would be leaving several long-distance telephone calls had been made to advertising managers with whom Peter had contacts, and arrangements had been made for advertisements to be shown in several magazines.

"Did you have a successful afternoon?" asked Fraser politely as he drove through the gates and turned the car in the direction of Ardmont. The rain had stopped and the sun had appeared, a disc of pale yellow no bigger than the moon.

"Far more successful than I had hoped. It was lucky that Sarah had Peter Wright staying with her," answered Lisa, and went on to explain what had happened.

"Is Sandy thinking of taking you into partnership?" queried Fraser.

"I think he would like that ... although I'm not sure whether I want to be tied down in that way. I'd really prefer to freelance as a designer, you know, get commissions just as you do for yachts."

"That's a chancy business," he remarked. "You have to be very good if you're going to keep the wolf from the door."

"You've made it," she pointed out.

"But only since I came back to Ardmont to a business which was already established. And I don't make my living from my designs. I make it from building boats, any sort of boat, by maintaining them, storing and mooring them, and by occasionally transporting them."

"Are you going to transport Mr. Creddon's schooner for him?"

"Yes, I am."

"How?"

"By sailing it. What other way?"

"I thought it might come by freighter. Won't it be cold and stormy sailing at this time of the year?"

"Probably. It usually is," he said with a grin. "But you must remember this schooner has been until now a freighter itself and it has two hefty diesel engines in it to push it along, so it won't be necessary to sail all the time."

"Will you go for it personally?"

"Did you imagine I sat in the office down at the boatyard and twiddled my thumbs while someone else brought it?" he scoffed. "I've been sailing other people's boats since I was a lad, and one of the reasons why I'm in the business is because

I enjoy sailing and the sea. I wouldn't pass up a chance like this for anything. There's only one problem. Harry wants it here by March so that we can start on the alterations he wants doing to the layout below decks, and I haven't found a suitable housekeeper yet to take Mrs. Dobie's place, at least not one that I'd like to leave Johnnie with while he's still shaky after that accident."

Now was her chance to rush in and say she would mind Johnnie for him, but she hesitated. His change of attitude towards her since she had told him she was not interested in marriage had put her on guard. She was fast discovering that when he stopped being a hedgehog he could be a pleasant companion.

The charm of the devil. That was how Aunt Maud had described it, and she was beginning to understand what her aunt had meant. There was charm in the brief flash of his smile, in those sudden direct glances which he gave her when she was least expecting them, in the odd, off-beat compliments which he occasionally handed out. And because it was used so rarely and because it was allied to a ruggedly handsome face and a lithe muscular physique such charm was dangerous and powerfully effective. He would use it, she decided, when he wanted something badly.

It was difficult to quell her natural impulse to offer to look after Johnnie, but this time it had to be done. She would wait and see what happened for once instead of rushing in.

Aunt Maud's car was where they had left it. To Lisa's relief it started when Fraser turned the key in the ignition. He manoeuvred it for her so that it was facing Ardmont to make sure that the engine was running smoothly.

"Seems perfectly all right to me," he remarked as he stepped out of the car. "Are you sure you didn't pretend it was boiling just to scrounge a lift with me?"

"I would never stoop to such a trick," she returned haughtily, taking her place in the driver's seat.

One hand on the door handle ready to close it on her, he looked down at her. It was another slow, considering glance, lingering on every feature of her face causing the blood to tingle beneath her skin. Again she felt as if he had reached out and touched her and yet he had not moved.

"You rise beautifully, Red Smith," he mocked, banged the door shut and walked away to his own car.

CHAPTER V

FIRED with enthusiasm after her discussion with Sarah and Peter, Lisa lost no time in going to see Sandy the following day. Although it was Saturday and the mill was not working he was there, showing round a young woman whom he introduced as Ina Scott, a skilled tailoress who worked in Glasgow, home for the week-end to visit her parents. She had called at the mill that morning to ask where she could buy some tweed, and knowing her trade Sandy had had the presence of mind to invite her in and to ask her if she would be interested in working for him.

"I won't deny I'm interested," she said to Lisa. "I'd like fine to come back and live in Ardmont, I'm that fed up with the city, but d'ye think ye'll be having any business?"

"We have it already," said Lisa triumphantly, and proceeded to tell them about Sarah's demands for some clothes which she would model for them. Then she showed Ina the drawings of the suits. The woman bent over them and then exclaimed with delight.

"Could you make them fairly quickly?" asked Sandy.

"I could that," agreed Ina, her big brown eyes sparkling in her smooth cream-coloured face. "I wish I could start now."

"Why can't you?" demanded Lisa.

"Och, well, I'd have to give notice to my firm," began Ina cautiously.

"How long?" asked Sandy.

"A week, or I'll forfeit my wages."

"Forfeit them," said Sandy with uncharacteristic recklessness. "I'll make them up to you."

Ina looked from him to Lisa, biting her lower lip uncertainly.

"I know you, Sandy Lewis," she said at last, "and I think I can trust you, but I'm not so sure . . ."

"You can trust me too," put in Lisa quickly. "Think, Ina, if you do as he suggests you won't have to go back to Glasgow tomorrow. You'll be able to work here during the springtime instead of in the grimy city."

"I'll pay good bonuses, Ina," said Sandy.

"Och, the two of ye have me in such a tizzy I'm not knowing what to do," complained Ina laughingly, her hand over her ears.

"Then go home and think about it," suggested Sandy. "If you decide to join us come out to the farm on Sunday afternoon for tea. Lisa will be there. She's bringing her great-aunt – you know Miss Roy, surely."

"Aye, I know Miss Roy. Are you her niece's daughter, then? I didna' ken that. But it makes all the difference."

Sandy nodded, smiling as if he understood her obscure statement.

"Yes, Lisa is almost but not quite a local," he said.

"Then I'll away now, Sandy, to think about it, and I'll be letting ye know."

Ina turned up at the farmhouse on Sunday afternoon and shyly joined the company there. The problem of finding someone to make the suits for Sarah to model solved, Lisa spent most of the following week making patterns from her designs and helping Ina to cut out the material. She found the dressmaker a merry, good-hearted girl, quick and methodical in her work. The daughter of one of Sandy's weavers and the foreman at the boatyard, she would have become a weaver herself if she had not been tempted by the superficial attractions of city life to leave her home town.

"Och, ye ken how it is when you're young, Lisa," she confided. "Ye want to spread your wings to find out if the fellows in the city are any better than the ones at home. And then I used to think Ardmont was a dreary place in the winter time. There was only fun in the summer when the holiday makers came. We had to go all the way into Kilbride if we wanted to dance, so off I went to Glasgow to be apprenticed to a dressmaker."

"Do you find Ardmont any different now?" asked Lisa. "You seem glad enough to come back."

"It's changed a wee bit for the better. The mill and the boatyard have brought some of the younger people back and some newcomers too. Have ye met Mr. Lamont from the yard yet?"

Lisa admitted that she had.

"My dad and my brother Wally both work for him. Wally was apprenticed to boatbuilding under Dad when the syndicate owned the yard. He had just finished his apprenticeship when it was closed down and both he and Dad were out of work for a while. Aye, but they were glad when Mr. Lamont came back and got things going again. They both like him and won't hear a word said against him, and believe me, there's been some funny things said, what with not knowing who is his wife or where she is."

"I thought she was dead."

"That's what some say. But nobody knows for sure, because he's never talked about her, and he isn't the one you'd ask questions of, so they tell me."

"No, he isn't," agreed Lisa quietly.

The possibility that Fraser's wife might still be alive bothered Lisa intermittently all day. The week had been so busy that she had not been able to do anything about Johnnie. But the boy had often been in her thoughts and as she drove home that evening she remembered him telling her that they had left his mummy in Tasmania.

Acting on impulse, she drove straight to the boatyard instead of turning up the brae to Breck House. It had been a bright boisterous day with sunlight glinting on the flurried water of the kyle and pageants of purple and white clouds rolling across the sky. As she walked over to the white house the wind twitched at her scarf and lifted the skirt of her cloak.

The front door was opened, not by Fraser as she had expected, but by a tall plump woman. Lisa recognized her at once as someone she had seen several times in the village.

"Is Mr. Lamont in?" she asked.

"Och, no, miss. He's awa' on the morning boat for Gourock."

"Oh. I really came to enquire about Johnnie."

"He's doing fine, but he's sleeping just now. Ye wouldn't want me to wake him, would ye?" said the woman anxiously. "He carried on that much after his dad had gone that he exhausted himself."

Lisa took a swift inventory of the woman. She looked clean and wholesome enough, and kindly too. Johnnie could not possibly come to harm with her.

"No, don't wake him," she said. "I'm Lisa Smith. I live in the house up the brae."

"I recognise ye. Ye're Miss Roy's niece. I'm Ellen Dixon. I said I'd look after Johnnie for the week. He was at his wits' end looking for someone to mind the child while he's awa' to Portugal."

"Well, I won't stay now, Mrs. Dixon, but if you should need any help with Johnnie please don't hesitate to ring me up. He knows me and we're good friends."

"Thank ye, miss. Maybe ye'll call in and see him then. It would help take his mind off his dad being away. Poor wee soul, he's bound to be upset. His dad is the only family he has, although I'm a wee bit sorry for the man too. It can't be easy being an only parent, for all he seems so strong and competent."

It was a new slant on Fraser, thought Lisa, as she sat later in Aunt Maud's bedroom sketching a new design. She had never considered the difficulties he must face being the only parent of a lively, sensitive child. How had he felt leaving Johnnie with Mrs. Dixon? Did he worry about the child while he was away? Lisa shook her head. She was putting feelings where there were none. Fraser was as hard as nails. He must be if he could go away so soon after Johnnie had been ill, just because he wanted to sail a boat across the sea.

"What are you muttering about?" asked Aunt Maud, rousing out of the light doze into which she had fallen. She had not been well that week and Lisa had had to ask the district nurse to call again. "You're getting as bad as I am for talking to yourself!"

"I was wondering how Fraser can bring himself to leave Johnnie and go away for so long," replied Lisa, and went on to describe how upset the boy had been when his father had left.

"Ach, don't be fretting over the bairn. Agnes Dixon is one of the best. He'll be fine with her. I wouldn't put it past the little rascal to play up when he knows his father is going away. Aye, it's a hard job rearing a child single-handed. He should get married again."

"Maybe he hasn't found the right person to marry."

"Humph, shouldn't be difficult. There's many a woman would be glad to look after a child in return for home and security. It would give the child a sense of security too when his father goes away instead of having to adjust to different baby-sitters."

"Probably you're right. But in these days a woman doesn't have to marry to get a home. And what about love, doesn't that come into it?"

"What's wrong with a marriage of convenience? Often they turn out better than the sort based on so-called love," growled Aunt Maud.

"Why did you never marry?" asked Lisa.

"Because the man I wanted to marry preferred someone else, that's why."

"But I thought you were engaged to be married."

"Aye, I was," sighed Aunt Maud. "To John Lamont, great-grandfather of your wee Johnnie. So now you know why I can't stand the sight of yon rascal Fraser. He's the image of John when I was engaged to him."

The week-end passed quietly. The Lewises came for tea and Sandy and Lisa took the dogs walking on the moors.

"Your aunt doesn't seem very well, although I can tell she's easier in her mind," said Sandy as they stopped to lean against an outcrop of granite and gaze down at the view.

"Yes, she does seem less harassed since Fraser told her he had no intentions of buying The Moorings now. I wish I knew what made him change his mind. All he would say was that he's no longer desperate for space since he received permission to build that new shed and he can afford to bide his time."

They both stared down at the shed which was now ready to have its roof put on.

"My father and Miss Roy have made Fraser appear like a monster who would devour Ardmont in one huge swallow," murmured Sandy musingly. "Whereas in actual fact he's only a man trying to do his best to improve his business and help the community. If Ardmont is to survive there have to be changes, but the older people here can't accept that. Don't let your outlook be infected by them, Lisa. Fraser needs all the friends he can find."

"What makes you say that?"

"Sometimes I have the feeling he's very lonely. Unlike me he doesn't have the help of a family ... or a very pretty partner."

"Two partners," she chipped in, laughing. "Remember we have Ina now."

"How could I forget her? No, Fraser's done everything on his own without anyone's help, and I admire him for what he's done. I couldn't have done it without encouragement and a helping hand ... like this one." He lifted her gloved hand from her side and pulled it through his arm. "Shall we go on, Lisa?"

She knew he was referring to their walk, but she had a sudden fear that perhaps he meant more, that he wanted her to go on with him through life, giving him a helping hand.

Her wild freedom-loving heart jibbed at the idea. Making a pretence of having to pull her hat on more securely, she removed her hand from the crook of his elbow and turned away to whistle up the dogs.

"We're ready to have a fitting with Sarah, now," she said

as she fell into step with him again, knowing that a conversation about the business would be safe ground. "Would you mind if I ask her to come to the mill tomorrow?"

"I don't mind you asking her, but she won't be coming, because she isn't at Creddon Hall. She's gone to Portugal with her father. They flew there yesterday. I met Mrs. Chisholm at church this morning and she was telling me."

"That's where Fraser has gone," she said, and her voice sounded strangely flat and dull.

"So I believe. Looks as if he might have found a stepmother for Johnnie sooner than anyone expected, doesn't it? Sarah is very hard to resist when she's persistent."

"Don't you mind?"

"Not at all. Why should I when I have you . . . and Ina, of course," he laughed, taking her hand in his again, and this time she did not pull it away.

Her conscience pricking her with regard to Johnnie, Lisa called in to see him on Monday afternoon. The weather had calmed down temporarily and the day was mild and sunny. Already coltsfoot were appearing shyly through the dead leaves under the hedges and snowdrops nodded their dainty heads in the garden at Breck House. Spring was on its way, slowly, inexorably. There would be a few setbacks between now and May, but nothing could stop the steady climb of the sun up the sky and the gradual wakening of nature.

Johnnie looked better than she had expected and seemed quite happy with Mrs. Dixon, whom he called Dixie. He talked for a while about his stay in hospital and the fun he had had with his father before Fraser had gone away. Then turning large reproachful eyes in her direction he said.

"Why didn't you come to see me before? I thought you were my friend."

"I am your friend, Johnnie, and I always will be. I couldn't come because I've been busy . . ."

"That's what Daddy said when I asked him. I thought perhaps you hadn't come because you were afraid of him. You

93

needn't be afraid, you know. He's quite kind when you get to know him."

Hiding a smile, Lisa promised to call the next day and to bring the dominoes.

She called every day after that, but on Thursday Mrs. Dixon met her with a worried expression on her face.

"I've just heard from Jeannie that Mr. Lamont has been delayed. The boat isn't quite ready. It means he won't be back until next Wednesday and I told him I could only stay until Monday."

"Can't Jeannie mind him?" suggested Lisa.

"Not really, miss. She has her own family, and between you and me, Johnnie doesn't care for her all that well."

"Where do you have to go on Monday?"

"I'm going to Gourock on the boat, to stay with my daughter's bairns. She's going into hospital for an operation."

"Then don't worry about it. If Mr. Lamont isn't back by then I'll keep Johnnie with me."

"That's a load off my mind. He's such a sweet wee laddie that I wouldn't like to upset him any more than I need. I can see that he likes ye and that'll he'll feel happy with you. By rights he should be going back to school by Monday. The doctor says there's no reason why he shouldn't."

Lisa decided not to tell Aunt Maud that she would be looking after Johnnie until Monday came because of the possibility that Fraser might be back. But when she heard the weather forecast for the Channel and the Irish Sea on Sunday evening predicted gale force winds she guessed that the schooner from Portugal would not be dropping its anchor in Ardmont Bay on Monday, so she went down to see Johnnie off to school and to assure him that she would meet him that afternoon, then went to break the news to Aunt Maud.

"You'll bring him here to sleep," insisted Aunt Maud.

"No, I thought I'd go down there."

"And have all of Ardmont gossiping? I'll not have you sleeping in Fraser Lamont's house. Besides, I need you here."

Johnnie was delighted at the idea of sleeping at Breck

House and helped Lisa pack his pyjamas, clean clothes and a few toys quite happily. In the small bedroom under the eaves next to Lisa's he was a little bothered by the sound of the wind as it soughed around the house and rattled the slates, so she stayed with him for a while and told him about her mother who had lived at Breck House and had slept in a room just like his.

"I'm sleeping in it just now, and I often think of her and one of the poems she used to say to me," she said.

"Say it to me," demanded Johnnie.

" 'I remember, I remember
The house where I was born,
The little window where the sun came peeping in at morn,
He never came a wink too soon
Nor brought too long a day . . .' "

Lisa's voice trailed away and she did not finish the verse from Thomas Hood's poem because Johnnie had fallen asleep.

All next day the wind blew and when Johnnie went to bed anxiety was obvious in his strained eyes.

"Does the sun really peep in your window in the morning, Lisa?" he asked after she had said the verse of the poem at his request.

"Yes, it does. In this one too, I expect, because they both face east."

"I didn't see it this morning because the sky was all grey and cloudy. Do you think the wind will stop blowing soon?"

"I hope so."

"I wish Daddy wouldn't go sailing," he sighed plaintively, voicing the anxiety which was uppermost in his mind, and to take his mind off the subject she said another poem to him.

In the night Lisa woke in sudden fright to the sound of Johnnie's voice calling her. She found him sitting up in bed sobbing.

"I dreamed that Daddy was drowned," he cried.

"Dreams often go by opposites, Johnnie. I expect he's quite safe in harbour somewhere," she murmured comfortingly as she straightened the bedclothes. She sat on the bed holding his hand and when she thought he had gone to sleep she would have crept out of the room, but his hand clutched at hers and he whispered,

"Don't go away."

So she lay down on the bed beside him and listened to the wind howling, her eyes wide in the darkness as she thought how awful it would be if Fraser were drowned at sea as his father had been drowned when he was a boy.

Lisa wakened suddenly. Her feet were cold because she had fallen asleep lying beside Johnnie without any bedclothes over her. She lay for a moment blinking drowsily at the chink of pale light which appeared at the curtained window trying to make out what was different.

Then she realised how quiet it was. The wind no longer rattled at doors and windows searching for an entrance to the house. The early morning was peaceful and slumbrous.

Suddenly, outside in the garden, a bird began to sing, a vigorous flutelike song. Another joined it, chirruping merrily as it welcomed the dawn, and soon the whole garden was alive with song.

Lisa slipped out of bed and tiptoed to the window to pull one of the curtains aside. Dawn had broken in the sky above the dark hump of the island of Boag and pale light was reflected in the water of the kyle which was still flecked by little foam-topped waves churned up by the recent wind.

Everything looked as it looked every morning. But there was one difference, a difference which set her heart thumping unaccountably and caused a flush to stain her cheeks. Dark against the water, nodding at its anchor chain, its two masts swaying slightly as it shifted on the changing tide, was a big black schooner.

Lisa did not question the impulse which sent her scurrying from Johnnie's room to her own. There she flung off her nightdress and dressed hastily in pants, tunic and shoes. Taking a belted suede jacket from the wardrobe, she pulled it on and dashed down the stairs along the hall and out of the house. The chilly morning air stung her face as she ran down the path, flung the gate wide and rushed out on to the road.

As she hurried she was conscious of a wonderful exhilaration. No wonder the birds were singing! She felt at one with them. Her heart was singing too.

"My heart is like a singing bird." How well that poem described how she felt this morning. But why?

Perhaps she would find the answer in the rest of the poem if she could remember it. Her run slowed to a walk as she searched her memory and she came to a full stop outside the entrance to the boatyard as the last line of the first verse of the poem leapt to her mind.

"Because my love is come to me."

Ridiculous! That might have been the reason for Christina Rossetti's heart being like a singing bird, but it was no reason for Lisa Smith's joyous mood because she had no love to come to her.

Then what was she doing here at the entrance to the boatyard at six o'clock on a chilly March morning?

She had come to make sure that Fraser was really back home and to tell him that Johnnie had cried for him in the night. She had come to ask him to reassure the child as soon as possible. That was the only reason.

But she could have waited. She could have taken breakfast first before telephoning cautiously and sedately. There was no need for this headlong rush.

She took a deep breath of the fresh cold air in an attempt to calm her singing heart and to quell her suddenly tumultuous thoughts. When she had recovered a semblance of her poise she walked through the yard up the steps of the house and inserted the key which Mrs. Dixon had left with her in the lock of the front door.

The key turned, the lock slid back and she opened the door and entered. The house was quiet and yet possessed that indefinable atmosphere that a house has when there is someone in it.

She peeped into the kitchen. There was no one there. Coming back into the hallway, she peered up the stairs. She would look in the big bedroom which Johnnie had told her was his father's to make sure Fraser was there and then she would go as quietly as she had come.

Upstairs all the doors were closed except one. She went over to it and peeped round it. In the pale morning light coming through the uncurtained window she could see quite clearly a tumble of dark hair on the pillow and the hump of a body under the bedclothes.

Backing out carefully, she pulled the door after her. To her consternation it creaked a little. She stood perfectly still hoping that it had not awakened Fraser, but her hope was unfulfilled.

"Is that you, Johnnie?" His voice sounded sleepy, benign. She did not answer or move, feeling sure he could hear the silly thumping of her heart.

"Johnnie." This time the whip crackled. "Come in here."

She put her head round the door and said as coolly as she could, "It's me . . . Lisa."

He sat up quickly. The bedclothes fell away from his shoulders. A few days' growth of beard made an Elizabethan buccaneer of him. The top buttons of his pyjamas were undone so that an expanse of chest was revealed. His generally dishevelled appearance made him seem vulnerable, more approachable.

Just how wrong she was about that was shown when he leaned back against the headboard of the bed and said coldly,

"Since when have you had the run of this house?"

How like him to put her in the wrong, she thought furiously, and her heart stopped singing abruptly.

"I . . . I came to make sure you're really back home and that the schooner out there isn't a figment of my imagination."

His eyebrows drew together in a perplexed frown.

"Why?"

"Because Johnnie is at Breck House."

"What is he doing there? Have you kidnapped him again?"

Recalling his jeer that she rose easily to baiting, she quelled an urge to retort rudely and answered with forced patience,

"Mrs. Dixon couldn't stay any longer. She had to go and look after her daughter's children, so I said I'd mind him. There was no way we could get in touch with you to ask your permission."

Reacting to the touch of acidity in her voice, he gave her a sharp glance.

"It would seem I'm in your debt," he said stiffly. "What does Miss Roy think of having my brat under her roof?"

"It was her idea that he should stay at Breck House. She didn't want me to sleep in your house – as if that would have mattered for two nights."

"It would have mattered, especially since I was back about one o'clock this morning," he replied gravely.

"Didn't you look in Johnnie's room?"

"The door was closed and I assumed he was asleep and didn't want to disturb him or Mrs. Dixon. How is he?"

"He's well, but he was very upset last night when he heard the wind howling. He had a bad nightmare. He dreamt you were drowned. Will you come to see him and assure him that you're alive?"

"Give me fifteen minutes and I'll be over at Breck House," he said brusquely. He flung back the bedclothes and Lisa retreated hastily, closing the bedroom door behind her.

As he had promised Fraser was no more than fifteen minutes in following her to Breck House, having dressed in his usual working clothes but not having stopped to shave.

Lisa's gaze lingered on the dark stubble of beard as she let him into the house.

"Johnnie won't know you like that," she murmured.

His fingers rasped against his chin as he rubbed the beard with one hand.

"Yes, he will. He's seen me with a beard before, in fact more with than without. Where is he?"

Lisa led him up the stairs, coping with an unfamiliar pang

of jealousy as she realised there was so much of his past life which she did not know about.

Johnnie was awake blinking drowsily in the dim light of his room. His greeting of his father was ecstatic and Lisa stayed in the room only long enough to pull back the curtains and see Fraser rumple his child's hair and speak to him in a cheerful familiar way which must have chased away all the boy's doubts and fears.

Downstairs again she busied herself with the preparation of breakfast, deliberately keeping her thoughts on her plans for the day. She would try to contact Sarah, who must be back at Creddon Hall by now. She hoped Sarah had not forgotten her promise to model the suits.

When she heard Fraser descending the stairs she went into the hall.

"Like some breakfast?" she asked casually, as he reached the bottom stair.

One hand resting on the newel post, he turned to look at her.

"The way to a man's heart?" he queried.

"Not at all," she retorted, forgetting she mustn't rise to his baiting remarks. "I'm merely being neighbourly. Anyway, I don't believe you have a heart, and even if you have the way to it must be strewn with sharp tacks making the approach to it most unpleasant, designed to deter the most determined and well-intentioned female, and not to be bypassed by the offer of ham and eggs, rolls and marmalade, coffee . . ."

"Say no more," he said, holding up a hand. "That's my favourite breakfast, provided you substitute tea for the coffee. As you assure me that you're well-intentioned I accept your offer."

Slightly suspicious of his mockery, Lisa turned away into the kitchen and he followed her.

"Do you know, you rant almost as well as Miss Roy," he said easily as he sat down in a chair at the table. "Have you been taking lessons, or is it a hereditary vice of the Roys?"

About to set a full plate in front of him, Lisa opened her mouth to retaliate, saw the twinkle in his eyes, closed her mouth again and set the plate down with exaggerated care.

"No more than I suspect that a tendency to tease and tantalise is a hereditary vice of the Lamonts," she said. "Is Johnnie getting up?"

"Not yet. I told him to stay put for another hour. He seems tired after his restless night," he replied, and began to eat.

"You must have had a very rough trip," she commented, sitting down opposite him. "We've had strong winds here for two days."

"I've known worse," he answered carelessly. "Fortunately we reached Campbelltown before it began to blow really hard, so we were in sheltered water all the way from there to here last night."

"Was the weather bad in Lisbon too? Was that why you were delayed?"

"No. Harry and Sarah seemed to think it was necessary to throw a couple of parties for their friends and acquaintances before we left," he said, and grinned reminiscently. "Sarah reminds me a little of Holly."

"Holly?" Lisa was puzzled.

He drank some tea before answering her.

"Johnnie's mother. She liked a gay time. The more people and parties the better."

Liked. He had used the past tense, so Holly must be dead. Almost holding her breath for fear she might destroy this moment of unexpected confidence, Lisa searched her mind for some way in which she could persuade him to tell her more about Johnnie's mother.

"Is Johnnie like her?" she asked gently.

"Yes. In more ways than one. Apart from his eyes he has her colouring," he replied, "and like her he's a little timid, afraid of the wind and the sea and of storms."

His mouth had taken on an unfamiliar scornful twist as if he could not understand such timidity in a child of his.

"Did you love her very much?" probed Lisa, still gently daring.

He flashed her a surprised glance, then his mouth tight-

101

ened into the usual proud straight line and she prepared herself to face a stinging retort.

"A woman's question," he jeered. "And the answer is I don't know."

"But you must know," she challenged. "You married her. Don't people usually marry for love?"

"So I've been told." His eyes and mouth were sceptical. "I didn't have time to find out. When I first met her Holly was pretty, fun to be with, hospitable. She was the only daughter of wealthy parents. I was lonely, a stranger in a strange land. She wanted to be married, so we married, against her parents' wishes. That was mistake number one. They cut us out of their lives."

"Why?"

He shrugged broad shoulders.

"They didn't say. I guess it was because they didn't consider me good enough for Holly. I was only a poor immigrant struggling to make my way in the boatbuilding industry in Hobart, whereas Holly was the daughter of one of Hobart's leading citizens, who had a private income of her own left to her by a doting grandmother. To their way of thinking no man was good enough for her."

He stopped talking to finish eating. Lisa gazed at his lean weatherbeaten face, thinking how much good breeding and pride of race were responsible for the clear-cut angles of nose and jaw, the fine wide sweep of brow above intelligent, direct eyes. The rest, the lines of humour and those of determination, were the product of his character. Oh, yes, Fraser Lamont, whether poor and struggling in Hobart, or successful and his own boss in Ardmont, was a man good enough for any woman, no matter how wealthy her parents might be.

"They thought you were a fortune-hunter," she suggested softly.

Humour glinted briefly in his eyes as he looked at her.

"Perhaps," he shrugged non-committally.

"What happened?"

"Their treatment of her made Holly very depressed. Then

102

we had Johnnie, which was mistake number two. Apparently she should never have had a child – a fine thing to find out after the event! She died twelve months after we'd been married, leaving her private income in trust for Johnnie when he comes of age."

"I'm sorry," whispered Lisa, slightly shocked by his curt, emotionless explanation of tragedy.

"Be sorry for Johnnie, not for me," he replied coldly, pushing her sympathy away. "He doesn't know what it's like to have a mother."

"And you like the world to think you don't mind not having a wife," accused Lisa sharply.

He leaned back in his chair and eyed her narrowly.

"I'd like to know just what lies behind that remark," he challenged.

"Dislike."

"Of me?" He didn't seem unduly perturbed by the possibility that she might dislike him.

"Dislike of your abominable pride which won't let you admit that you loved Holly and regretted her death, or that you need someone to be a mother to Johnnie. You're so afraid someone might pity you."

The colour put there by exposure to strong winds and inclement weather seeped away from his face, leaving it taut and pale. For a few seconds his eyes blazed blue murder at her and she leaned back away from him, thinking he might strike her.

But his anger was short-lived. His eyes narrowed again and black eyelashes hid the expression of violence. Rising to his feet, he pushed the chair carefully under the table and stood looking down at her.

"You know you should be careful what you say, Red Smith," he drawled, "or I'll be getting the wrong impression again. Such interest on your part in me and the way I should or shouldn't feel might lead me to think that you're angling to be Johnnie's stepmother yourself, in spite of what you told me the day we went to Creddon Hall."

Appalled that she had left herself so wide open for such

a crack, Lisa could only stare up at him, her heart no longer as light as a bird's, but heavy, heavier than the customary lead.

"Thanks for the breakfast," he was saying crisply, "and for looking after Johnnie. Perhaps you wouldn't mind seeing him off to school for me. I've a lot to do today as we must get the schooner out of the water before the weather deteriorates again. Tell Johnnie to come to the yard when he comes home and I'll see him there."

He had gone before she had recovered. Then, urged by the desire to explain, to apologise for what she had said, Lisa hurried after him and reached the front door, only to have it slammed in her face. She opened it. All the glory of the sunrise, orange and rose-tinted cirrus cloud fanning out against the azure sky above the dark hump of Boag, blazed before her eyes.

The iron gate clanged as Fraser swung it shut behind him. Lisa ran to it and leaned over it.

"Fraser!" she called, and knew he must have heard her. He did not look back but continued to walk steadily down the narrow road along which she had run so blithely only an hour earlier. And something about the set of his shoulders and the determined thump of his feet on the surface of the road made her realise the futility of following him. It was quite obvious he wanted nothing to do with her.

If Sarah mentioned Fraser's name again, she would scream, thought Lisa, later the same day. As she had hoped, the model had returned to Creddon Hall and had been quite willing to come to the mill to have the clothes made for her fitted. She had been at the mill for over an hour now, standing patiently while Ina fitted skirts and jackets, or sitting and smoking while an alteration was made to an article.

And all the time she had talked about Portugal and the fun she had had there with Fraser. Several times Lisa had tried to change the subject, conscious of Ina's pricked ears, knowing how furious Fraser would be if his visit to Portugal with Harry Chisholm and his daughter became the subject of gossip all over the Ardmont peninsula. But inevitably Sarah returned to her favourite theme.

"Is that the last one?" she yawned, as she stepped carefully out of a skirt and handed it to Ina. "Good, that leaves me time to drive down to the slip to see if the schooner is out of the water."

She dressed quickly in her own clothes, a close-fitting tunic with a mandarin collar, flared pants and high-heeled shoes.

"I wanted to sail back," she announced as she attended to her make-up.

"I thought you didn't like sailing," said Lisa.

"I don't, but I'd have put up with anything to come back with Fraser. However, he wouldn't hear of it. He says he doesn't like having a woman on board and that he'd prefer to find me waiting here, looking decorative. I didn't press him because I know I'm decorative and that I like nothing better than being in the forefront of a reception committee, especially if there's someone like Fraser to be welcomed."

"It's a pity you weren't at the boatyard about one o'clock this morning, then," said Lisa, with an acidity which surprised even herself and was not lost on Sarah, who pouted a little as she replied,

"Well, I couldn't help that. He told me he wouldn't be arriving until this afternoon. How was I to know he'd get here sooner? But better late than never. I'll go and welcome him now."

She went off and for a while there was silence in the room. Lisa stared out of the window, recalling the welcome Fraser had received from herself. Hardly a hero's welcome, she thought with a grin. They had circled round each other verbally, like two angry cats spitting suspicion and snarling home truths. Yet when she had set out for the boatyard she had been so full of gladness because he had come back safe and sound. Gladder than a singing bird.

"So that was Sarah Popham," said Ina. "I canna say I'm impressed."

"She's very good as a model," replied Lisa.

"That's as maybe," said Ina grudgingly. "Seemed to me she was laying it on awful thick about her high jinks in Portugal."

"You won't repeat anything she said, Ina, please? Mr. Lamont would be very annoyed if it became the subject of gossip in the village."

"No, I won't. I'm not a spreader of exaggerations."

"Exaggerations?" repeated Lisa, a mystified expression on her face.

"That's what I meant by her laying it on thick. Och, ye're awful innocent when it comes to dealing with other women, Lisa. She was exaggerating and extending everything that happened while she was in Portugal. I've heard a lass do it before when she's wanted to impress another lass and make her jealous. She'd make out she'd had such a good time with a fellow when if the truth were known he'd been quite disinterested in her."

"But who would Sarah be trying to impress today?"

"Well, it wasna' me, I can tell ye that, because I dinna know Mr. Lamont," said Ina with a grin. "Could only be you," she added, as she went out of the room.

Had Sarah been exaggerating her relationship with Fraser? wondered Lisa as she went back to Breck House in the clear light of late afternoon. Had the model intended to irritate her and make her jealous? Because if that had been her intention she had succeeded. For a while in the room at the mill she had been swamped by a green tide of jealousy because Sarah had danced with Fraser, had laughed with him and had been asked by him to be decorative and waiting for him when he returned from sea.

Why should she feel jealous, an emotion she had rarely experienced in the whole of her life until now? And why should Sarah Popham want to make her jealous? There was nothing between herself and Fraser to make Sarah think she had competition.

Nothing? Could she be sure of that?

She lingered in the front garden enjoying the softness of the

106

air and the warmth of the sunlight, pretending she was more interested in the crocuses just showing purple and yellow through the grass than she was in the two figures inspecting the new shed. Sarah's honey-coloured hair gleamed in the sunlight as she swung it back from her face and the top of her head reached just to Fraser's shoulder.

Nothing between herself and Fraser! What about the flare of attraction she had felt coming back from Creddon Hall? What about the anxiety which had racked her during the night when like Johnnie she had imagined Fraser drowned? What about her singing heart that morning? But what about the slanging matches they had had? Didn't they prove something too?

Never heard of the couples who expressed their love for each other in verbal warfare? she argued with herself. Like Beatrice and Benedick in *Much Ado About Nothing*, who had loved each other against their wills?

It couldn't be true. She couldn't be in love. She didn't want to be in love, and certainly not with a tough self-contained character like Fraser, who had admitted he had not known whether he had loved his first wife or not.

No, this feeling was foolish, the sort indulged in by romantic ex-schoolgirls like Marjorie Morrison, unworthy of the freedom-loving independent woman she knew herself to be, and it must be squashed at all costs.

However, during the next few days she had little time to indulge in the feeling. A cable arrived from her father stating that he had three months' leave and that he intended to spend some time with her at Breck House. He would arrive at Prestwick Airport the following Saturday morning and hoped that she would meet him there.

"Just like Frank Smith," grumbled Aunt Maud. "Always last minute. Thinks we have nothing better to do but wait about for him to come home on leave. Expects you drop everything and run to meet him. You'll have to go over on Friday and stay the night in Prestwick. You'd better ask Isabel to come and stay the night with me."

"That's the day Peter Wright is arriving. He's going to photograph Sarah at Creddon Hall. I promised I'd take Ina there on Saturday to make sure the clothes are fitted right," said Lisa.

"It might rain," comforted Aunt Maud, "then they'll have to postpone the photography. They'll just have to manage without you for once. It'll not do them any harm. Sandy Lewis is beginning to depend on you too much lately. He's making a lot of demands on your time."

"Oh, I don't think of him as demanding. I like designing for him. He's so appreciative."

"Humph. Doesn't do to be at a man's beck and call, as you should know. He'll start getting ideas if you are."

"Such as?" prompted Lisa, who was always interested in her aunt's views on the opposite sex.

"He might start thinking you're in love with him. Are you?"

"Good heavens, no!" exclaimed Lisa. "Whatever makes you think that?"

"The way you've been behaving lately. Reminds me of your mother when she first knew Frank."

Alarmed by Aunt Maud's shrewd observation, Lisa jumped to her feet and walked over to the window. The new shed was now covered by a roof. She could see Fraser standing, hands on his hips, his head tilted back as he talked to one of the men still working on the roof. The sight of his straight compact figure made her pulses race and the blood burned in her cheeks. She curved both hands round her face in an attempt to cool it.

"What have I been doing that's odd?" she queried in a slightly creaky voice.

"Just what you've done now. Jumping out of your chair for no apparent reason. Staring out of the window. Standing in the garden absent-mindedly stripping my lilacs of their new buds. Rising with the dawn and rushing off down the road. Och aye, ye needn't deny it, lass – I've watched you and I've heard you. And what's more, you get into the middle of a sentence, then forget what you're going to say and go off into a dream. Sure sign of being in love."

"Did my mother really behave like this when she met Dad?" asked Lisa softly.

A small figure had joined Fraser, a boy with blond hair who tugged at his father's sweater to get his attention. Fraser looked down at him and a few seconds later they walked away from the shed towards the yard.

"Aye, she did," sighed Aunt Maud. "You're like her in many ways. More generous than I ever was. I hope no man ever takes advantage of you."

"Do you think Dad took advantage of Mother?" asked Lisa, a dangerous edge to her voice. She loved her father dearly and even her liking for Aunt Maud would not allow her to stand by and hear him vilified.

"No," replied Aunt Maud smoothly. She could be diplomatic when she wanted. "But I think you should be on guard against those who might take advantage of your generosity, and use it for their own selfish ends."

When Lisa told Sandy that she would be unable to go to Creddon Hall he offered to go himself and take Ina with him.

"I'll do anything for you, Lisa," he said lightly. "After all, that's what a partner is for, to share the load."

"But I'm not a partner yet."

"That's true. I wish you would decide to join us. Working with you has made all the difference to me. But you must know that. Seeing you here, listening to you talking enthusiastically about design has given me a new, fresh outlook on life and on the tweed industry." His faintly self-disparaging smile which never failed to rouse her desire to take him by the shoulders and shake him out of his lack of self-esteem appeared. "I was in danger of becoming slightly sour, not having known success either in business or love. You've changed all that."

"I have?" she wondered uneasily, her gaze flickering to the door of his office as she contemplated escape.

To her relief the door opened and Ina stepped briskly into the room. Over one arm she was carrying a tweed suit.

"I thought ye'd like to be seeing the first one," she said, her brown eyes flicking from Lisa's face to Sandy's and back again as if she sensed a certain tension between them. She laid the suit on the desk and stood back proudly to admire her own handiwork.

"It's perfect, Ina," said Lisa. "Just imagine how marvellous it's going to look on Sarah."

"Aye, I'm looking forward to seeing her in it. What time d'ye want me to be ready on Saturday morning?"

Lisa explained that Sandy would be going to the castle instead of herself, and was surprised to see a gleam of warm pleasure light up Ina's eyes.

"Och, then that's just fine. And what time would you be wanting to leave Sandy? Sure and I never thought I'd ever be going to Creddon Hall as a guest with the owner of Ardmont Mill to see me own sewing being photographed," exclaimed the little seamstress, and while she and Sandy made their arrangements for Saturday Lisa slipped out of the room, thankful that once more she had avoided a serious personal conversation with Sandy.

CHAPTER VI

THE Boeing 707 in which Frank Smith had flown across the Atlantic Ocean landed on time early on a bright blustery March morning. He came through the door from the Immigration and Customs department, tall and spare, impeccably dressed as always, the white flashes in his dark well-groomed hair emphasised by the tan he had acquired during six years in the Caribbean. When he saw Lisa he dropped the hand-luggage he was carrying, put his arms round her and held her closely for a moment.

Within two hours of his landing they were standing together on the top deck of the yellow-funnelled ferry-boat as it transported them across the Clyde, admiring the view of the mountains of Saddleback and the Cobbler to the north and the dark jagged peaks of the island of Arran to the south.

Frank did most of the talking, telling her about various experiences during his work with the British Trade Commission in the Caribbean, and it was not until they were passing the low-lying craggy islands at the narrows of the kyle that Lisa told him about Aunt Maud's poor health and how the worry over keeping Breck House had brought her low.

"Why is she worried?" asked Frank calmly.

"Wait. You'll see in a few minutes as we approach Ardmont pier," replied Lisa.

And he did see and stared in amazement at the mushroom growth of sheds at the boatyard which seemed, from this point of view, to be encroaching on Breck House, trying to push the old house off its land.

"Good lord!" he exclaimed mildly. "Looks as if the yard is booming. If I'm not mistaken that's a new fishing vessel being built over there. Didn't know they built stuff like that. Who owns the place now?"

"A man called Lamont."

111

"Oh, so it's back in the family. Can't be Charlie Lamont. He was drowned over twenty years ago, before you were born. Nice chap. Not much of a head for business . . . too kindly. He was always ready to do someone a good turn. I hired a dinghy from him that time I spent a holiday here when I first met your mother. He had a boy, tough little blighter, afraid of nothing. Could sail anything."

"He's still like that," drawled Lisa. "He's the Lamont I'm talking about. But I'll let Aunt Maud tell you about him."

Later that day Frank lounged before the fire in the sitting room at Breck House and listened to Aunt Maud, who had made an effort to come downstairs to greet him, as she complained about Fraser Lamont.

"Do you know, I'm thinking I preferred it when I knew what he was going to do," she grumbled finally. "Then I could take action to block him. But this recent idea of his to bide his time until he gets what he wants is more worrying. I feel like a mouse being played with by a cat, wondering where he's going to pounce next."

"I'll go and have a talk with him while I'm here," said Frank. "Pump him a bit, diplomatically, of course. I can see why you're concerned, Maud, but I'm afraid you can't stop the march of time and progress."

"You call yon sheds progress?" she demanded.

"I'll admit they're not beautiful and I know it would be ideal if places like Ardmont could remain untouched. But if they're to be viable communities in this day and age they have to move with the times. There's a great demand for yachting facilities in these parts and you can't stop the man from cashing in on it. Personally I think he's to be admired for coming back here and making an effort to revitalise the industry," replied Frank equably.

"But why does he have to do it at the expense of my peace of mind?" growled Aunt Maud. "I've looked out at the kyle and at the islands for years, and now what do I see? Huge sheds blocking my view, and if he has his way he'll be on the other side too, squeezing me out. Lisa thought of putting in an offer for The Moorings to stop him from buying the place."

"Oh, indeed? And what were you going to use for money?" asked Frank with an amused glance at his daughter.

"I was going to ask you for a loan," she replied honestly.

"Don't you like Lamont either?" he asked idly.

"I . . . I . . ." began Lisa, appalled to hear herself stuttering hesitantly. She looked up warily to find she was being watched closely by two pairs of eyes, one sharp and disapproving, the other indulgently amused. She felt the colour drain from her face as she realised she was not prepared to divulge her opinion of Fraser to either her father or her aunt.

"I think it's time we had a hot drink," she added, recovering quickly, and springing to her feet, she sped from the room.

Although aware that he was very observant and extremely alert, Lisa found her father's presence in Breck House very comforting. Having spent all his working life in the British Civil Service in various trade commissions which had taken him to many different parts of the Commonwealth, he had developed a calm and collected attitude to life, totally lacking in prejudice. He was interested in everything and everyone, yet he rarely passed judgement on anyone.

While he was staying in Ardmont he was determined to see as much of his daughter as possible and so was not averse to accompanying her to the mill to be introduced to Sandy and Ina and to be shown round.

Ina was still full of her impressions of the day she had spent at Creddon Hall, and while Sandy was busy explaining the methods by which the wool was spun and carded she took Lisa aside to tell her all about the photographic session.

"Och, wait till ye see the photos, Lisa," she said. "They're going to be super. Sarah was right – the castle is a perfect setting for that type of clothing. We had a lovely time. Mrs. Chisholm gave us lunch and in the afternoon Mr. Lamont came. He was out to see Mr. Chisholm about the alterations to his schooner, and he brought his little boy with him. He was very interested in what we were doing."

"Och, I canna think when I've enjoyed meself so much. He's very nice when ye get to know him."

"Who is? Mr. Lamont?"

"Och, no, I mean Sandy, of course, although I can see why Sarah is keen on the other. He has a silent self-contained strength which would appeal to some women."

"But not to you."

"No. I like a man to be gentle and to treat me as if I'm something precious even if I'm not. There's nothing better for a woman's morale than to be treated like that, and mine certainly received a boost yesterday," said Ina with her gay laugh.

From Sandy, Lisa supposed, with a faint feeling of un-easiness. She could imagine the simple, practical Ina falling in love very hard with the first man who treated her gently, and she hoped she would not be hurt by Sandy who, she was beginning to realise, had a tendency to reach out for the un-attainable when it came to women.

Sandy's view of the visit to Creddon Hall was slightly dif-ferent from Ina's. As Lisa was about to leave the mill he drew her aside to glance at the layout of a brochure he was going to have printed.

"It's about the tweed and the sheepskins. We'll need some-thing like this to send out when we receive answers to the advertisements which will be appearing soon," he pointed out.

"Did Sarah agree to model sheepskins coats, too?" asked Lisa.

"I couldn't get a straight answer from her," he replied with a touch of irritation. "She kept flirting with the photographer and then when Fraser turned up she behaved as if she were out of her mind."

"And how did Fraser react?"

"Oh, with his usual indifference, which only had the effect of goading her to further idiotic behaviour. And then to crown everything Johnnie, who was very disappointed when he found you weren't there, kicked Sarah."

114

"Why?" asked Lisa, astounded by this evidence that her blond favourite was not always the sweet-tempered child she believed him to be.

"I felt like cheering when he did it," answered Sandy with a surprising touch of viciousness. "She deserved to be kicked for making a most unpleasant remark about you. Anyway, Fraser reprimanded him and took him off. Sarah stormed into the castle with Peter Wright following her and Ina and I came home for tea at her parents' home."

Lisa could not help smiling. His "Ina and I came home for tea" sounded so cosy and normal.

"It seems I missed an eventful afternoon," she murmured. "What was Sarah's unpleasant remark?"

Sandy looked distinctly embarrassed and began to shuffle papers together, avoiding her eyes.

"Something about Johnnie needing to take care where you're concerned, that you were only friendly with him because you wanted to use him to get close to his father ... and a lot of similar rubbish. None of us there believed a word she said. It was just spite." Sandy looked up from his papers and smiled diffidently at her. "I hope you'll bring your father to tea at the farm on Sunday. My parents remember him well and would like to meet him again. You and I can go for a walk if the weather is good. I've a great deal to say to you, Lisa." He glanced round the dusty office and added, "This isn't the time or the place."

The expression in his eyes would have boosted any woman's morale and set her heart thudding hopefully, thought Lisa. But the only effect it had on her heart was to make it flutter like that of a wild bird determined to preserve its freedom.

"Time and place aren't important, Sandy," she said. "It's what is said that matters."

He gave her an impatient glance.

"I can't agree," he replied. "There's something I must tell you and I don't want anyone else listening. It's important ... to me at any rate, and I hope it will be for you."

Well, at least she knew what to expect when she took a walk

115

with Sandy on Sunday next, thought Lisa with a touch of amusement, and knowing she would be able to take avoiding action and not give him an opportunity to declare himself. She was sure he was not in love with her but was only temporarily attracted to her because she was different and because she had helped him. She was beginning to understand now what Aunt Maud had meant when she had suggested that Sandy might be getting ideas. The more she helped him the more he would make demands, gradually assuming that she was there just for his benefit and eventually taking her for granted.

"Pleasant enough chap," said Frank suddenly. "He should go far with someone cracking the whip behind him. Has the basis of a fine little industry there."

"And who do you think will crack the whip?" asked Lisa, as she steered the car along the shore road. The water of the kyle was placid and serene, pale lavender colour shading to deep tones of violet and indigo under the cloud-streaked sky.

"That little nut-brown maid might be the one," mused Frank.

"You mean Ina?"

"Yes, I do. Unless you're thinking of taking him on yourself."

"If you mean by 'taking on' ... marriage ... nothing was ever further from my mind," replied Lisa. "I could only marry for love, and love is only possible between equals."

"And you haven't met yours yet, I take it," teased Frank, amused by her reaction. "Yes, now that I come to think of it whoever tames your wild heart will need to have a strong hand as well as a loving one."

Lisa glanced at him sharply. Shades of Beatrice and Benedick again! Wasn't it Beatrice, when learning that Benedick really loved her, who had said,

"And, Benedick, love on; I will requite thee;
Taming my wild heart to thy loving hand."

She was about to question her father, to ask him whether those were the lines he had in mind when he turned from his contemplation of the kyle and the shores of Boag and said,

"You're right, of course, love is only possible between equals. There's nothing new about that, as anyone who has been happily married and believes in marriage will tell you. But be careful, Lisa, that your love of freedom and independence doesn't prevent you from recognising your equal when he comes along. I wouldn't like you to miss him as Beatrice almost missed Benedick." He glanced out of the window at a small boy dressed in navy blue who was trudging along by the hedges, stepping into every puddle left by the recent rain, and who looked up hopefully as he heard the car approach. "Who's that?" asked Frank.

"Johnnie Lamont," replied Lisa, bringing the car to a halt just ahead of the smiling Johnnie, who came racing up and peered in through the window at Frank. "We'll give him a lift."

Frank opened the door, smiled at the boy, stepped out of the car, and swung his seat forward so that Johnnie could climb into the back seat.

Pink-cheeked and breathless, Johnnie started to talk as soon as the car started forward.

"I've something to give you, Lisa," he said, waving a rolled-up piece of thick paper. "It's a picture I made at school today."

Lisa, who had noticed his unfastened coat, his undone shoelaces and his wild, spiky hair, wondered if he had been fighting again.

"Thank you, Johnnie. That's very kind of you. I hope you haven't been in another fight," she said.

"Oh, no. Jamie and I have been rolling down the grass bank at the back of his house."

"Jamie?" queried Lisa.

"Jamie Carruthers. He's my new friend," he announced importantly. "His dad works for my dad."

Frank turned and looked at him, held out his hand and introduced himself.

117

"How do you do, Johnnie. I used to know your dad when he was a boy."

"I'm seven," replied Johnnie after solemnly shaking hands. "Was he as old as that when you knew him?"

"Older. About ten or eleven, I'd say."

"Have you been to see him?"

"Not yet. But I'd like to. I'd like to look at some of those yachts he's got in his yard."

"Come now," said Johnnie generously, having taken one of his instant likings. "I'll show you round," he added, assuming his own special adult manner. "You too, Lisa?"

Lisa shook her head as she stopped the car at the bottom of the brae.

"Not now, Johnnie. You get out and take Mr. Smith while I put the car in the garage." She unrolled the picture he had given her as he scrambled out of the car. It was a brightly crayoned drawing of a daffodil growing in a plant pot. "Thank you for the lovely drawing. I'll put it up on the wall in the kitchen at Breck House and then I can see it every day."

"Show it to Miss Roy, too," instructed Johnnie as he walked off with Frank, his hand in his, in the direction of the boatyard. Lisa sat and watched them for a minute before putting the car into gear and swinging it in the direction of Breck House.

She had decided not to go with her father and Johnnie to the boatyard, partly because she knew Frank wanted to talk to Fraser by himself and partly because she did not want to see Fraser. No, that was not exactly true. She was afraid to see him – afraid of that excited bubbling feeling which she experienced whenever she laid eyes on him. It was a feeling she attributed to purely physical attraction, to the time of the year. It would pass, she hoped, with the spring. Meanwhile she would help it on its way by playing safe.

The biggest problem was Johnnie. How to see him and remain friends with him without laying herself open for more sarcastic jibes from Fraser, punishing remarks which she could not forget, occupied her thoughts daily.

When Frank returned from the boatyard he seemed quite satisfied with his meeting with Fraser.

"I can't understand why you don't like him," he said to Aunt Maud. "He seems a reasonable, intelligent sort of chap to me; ambitious, hardworking, knows where he's going. No need for anyone to crack the whip behind him," he added, with a sidelong glance at Lisa.

"You're right there," commented Maud dryly. "It's the other sort of handling he needs ... a good hard pull on the reins to stop him from over-reaching himself. He'd buy up half Ardmont if he could."

"I think you're wrong," said Frank. "He just wants a bit more elbow room, and when he has that he'll be content." He produced his pipe and began to stuff it with tobacco, a favourite tactic of his when he did not want to be drawn into an argument.

"Ach, it's just like you to side with him," sneered Aunt Maud. "What else did you find out?"

"Nothing very much. He showed me his fibre-glass workshop and then took me to see a hull being built in the old traditional carvel style. I was pleased to see he's keen on keeping the old boat-building crafts alive even though he's gone in for mass-production. Craftsmen like Willie Scott and his son are worth every penny they earn. I told him something of the boat-building I'd seen being done in the Caribbean. Then he showed me the ocean-racer he's just finished for some chap who's interested in being chosen to represent the United Kingdom in the Admiral's Cup series. If that yacht's successful it'll boost Lamont's business no end."

"Ach, never mind all that," interrupted Aunt Maud irritably. "Did you get out of him what his next move concerning Breck House is?"

Frank gave her a slightly disdainful glance as if her impatience offended him.

"Good heavens, no! That will take time. I have to win his confidence before I start doing that. He was cagey enough as it was when he remembered who I was and my relationship to you and Lisa." Again he flicked a sharp shrewd glance in the direction of his daughter, whose cheeks suddenly glowed red for no accountable reason. "But I'll be seeing him again," continued Frank placidly. "The boy is a useful contact. Jolly little chap, but nervous and far too attached to his father. It's a pity he hasn't a mother."

"Fraser isn't the first man to bring up a child on his own these days," said Aunt Maud gruffly.

"Nor the last. But I got the impression today that he's feeling the strain a little."

"Oh, why?" The question was out of Lisa before she had time to think, and her father gave her another curious glance.

"He seemed unnecessarily irritable with the boy. Of course it could be that he has some problem on his mind," he replied.

In the days that followed Frank was often down at the boatyard, apparently fascinated by the activity there. He had taken over Lisa's former self-imposed task of meeting Johnnie as he came home from school and Lisa was glad to let him do so as it eased her conscience a little where the boy was concerned.

With regard to Fraser having a problem on his mind which was making him short-tempered she wondered whether it was connected with Sarah. If he was in love with Sarah and wanted to marry her Johnnie's dislike of the model could create almost insurmountable difficulty.

She was encouraged to think she was right by Sarah's own behaviour when she came to the mill one day, bringing with her two friends who were staying at Creddon Hall for a few days and who were interested in the tweeds. Sarah showed off all the time, taunting Lisa about her friendship with Johnnie and her relationship with Sandy. Her whole manner was brittle in the extreme as if she were on the verge of a nervous breakdown or hysteria.

"She's got it in for you, right enough," muttered Ina after the model and her friends had left. "She's fair wild about something. My guess is that she doesn't like ye being so friendly with the wee Lamont laddie when she knows he loathes the sight of her. She's afraid ye might cut her out with his dad."

Lisa laughed.

"As if I would or even could! I hardly ever see the man," she said.

That wasn't exactly true. She managed to see Fraser every day somehow, using every means she could think of to see him and not be seen — peeping from her bedroom window to watch him walk to the new shed, taking the setters for walks along the paths which climbed the hill at the back of the boatyard so that she could look down and see him crossing the boatyard. One day, greatly daring, she walked right past the entrance to the boatyard hoping she might see him giving instructions to the men working on the big schooner. He caught sight of her and paused in what he was saying to the workman leaning over the high stern of the boat. His eyes flicked over her in a quick slightly surprised way before he turned his back on her, deliberately, to continue with what he had to say.

And she had gone on, her legs strangely shaky, vowing to herself she would not pass that way again when he was there.

Secretly astounded by her own behaviour, Lisa found she could not help it. For once natural instinct was having its way with her, pushing aside the dictates of her will no matter how hard she tried to assert that strong and highly-developed faculty.

Sunday came round once more, a clear calm day. Walking with Sandy along the long rocky snout of land from which Ardmont got its name, she told him of her suspicions regarding the situation between Fraser and Sarah in order to prevent him from telling her the "something important" which he did not wish anyone else to hear.

"You could be right," he murmured, giving the matter his usual grave consideration as they paused at the end of point of land and looked out across the sea. On distant land hazy blue mountains basked serenely in the pale spring sunlight, the water twinkled happily and rushed at the shore in a series of merry little waves. "Sarah, of course, won't have any idea how to deal with a young boy like Johnnie," continued Sandy, then stopped abruptly and stiffened as he looked past her. "Better change the subject quickly, Lisa," he warned quietly. "Someone else has decided that today is a good day to walk round the point."

She turned slowly. Coming along the shore towards them were three familiar figures – Sarah and Fraser followed by a dawdling Johnnie. As soon as he saw Lisa Johnnie broke into a run, overtook the other two and dashing up to her held out a fistful of shells for her inspection.

Compared with his boisterous greeting of Lisa the four adults' greetings seemed remarkably constrained. With a cool nod and a politely-spoken "Fine day for the time of year," Fraser walked on indifferently. Sarah, however, did not possess his composure or his understanding of Johnnie, who would have followed his father eventually. She paused and said in a superficially sweet manner,

"Come along, Johnnie, dear. Lisa doesn't want to be bothered with those silly shells. She's taking a walk with Mr. Lewis."

"You do want to look at the shells, don't you, Lisa?" said Johnnie, looking up at her appealingly, and she saw bewilderment and hurt in his blue eyes and that his lower lip was quivering.

"Yes, I do," she replied, unable to resist that look, ignoring her initial intention to play on Sarah's side and suggest that the boy go with the other woman.

"Johnnie, hurry up," insisted Sarah peevishly.

"No. I don't have to do what you say," returned Johnnie. "I want to stay with Lisa and go for a walk with her."

"That's all very well, laddie," interposed Sandy mildly, "but Lisa and I happen to be going in the opposite direction to your father and Sarah, so it can't be done."

Sarah glared at him exasperatedly.

"Can't you see, Sandy Lewis, that it would be more helpful if you changed your mind and walked the other way? Then he'll come without any more fuss," she said, and Lisa waited tensely for his reply.

"Well, I suppose we could do that," he replied obligingly. "Would you mind, Lisa?"

Thinking that he would have even less chance to tell her "something important" now that Sarah was there, Lisa let her glance stray in the direction Fraser had gone. He had stopped walking and was waiting, hands in his pockets, staring out to sea.

"No, I don't mind. You go ahead. Johnnie and I will follow," she replied absently.

Sandy looked a little taken aback by her easy acquiescence, but before he could suggest any alternative Sarah had linked an arm through his and was saying gaily,

"Come on, Sandy. It won't be the first time you and I have walked along this shore together."

They went off, and Fraser having noticed that they were approaching turned and began to walk slowly in the direction of the village.

Johnnie looked up at Lisa with a conspiratorial grin which showed his two new, slightly crooked, top front teeth.

"Now I've got you to myself," he said triumphantly. "Oh, look! A little crab. Help me catch him, Lisa."

It took some time for Lisa to persuade Johnnie that they were not going to catch the crab that day, and by the time they reached the end of the village Sandy and Sarah had disappeared and only Fraser was there, leaning against the gate set in the dry stone dyke which divided the Lewises' farm fields from the shore. He watched them come, a rather forbidding frown on his face.

"You two have taken long enough," he said reprovingly, as he straightened up.

"Where are the others?" asked Lisa, trying to appear indifferent to this unexpected encounter.

"Sandy invited Sarah to tea at the farm. He said to tell you to follow them over the fields." He jerked his head in the direction of the path on the other side of the gate.

"Didn't he invite us to tea too, Daddy?" asked Johnnie brightly. "I'd like to go to the farm and see the animals."

"Yes, he did, but I refused on your behalf," replied Fraser curtly. "The way you've behaved this afternoon you don't deserve to go to tea anywhere."

Johnnie's shoulders slumped, tears of disappointment welled in his eyes and Lisa decided it was time to interfere.

"Oh, why don't you come? I'm sure Mrs. Lewis won't mind. There's always plenty to eat, and Mr. Lewis loves to show off his barns and his equipment," she said persuasively.

The glance Fraser gave her was both cynical and hostile.

"Can you imagine Hugh Lewis sitting down at his own table in comfort with me as his guest? Or Maud Roy enjoying her afternoon out having to face me across the tea-cups?" he asked derisively. "No, thank you. I would rather not go where I know I'm not welcome. Come on, Johnnie. It's a long walk back through the village."

Without a word of farewell to Lisa he turned away and set off. Johnnie hesitated, looking up at Lisa. Realising the boy was not following him, Fraser swung round.

"Johnnie!" he called harshly.

"I want to go with Lisa to tea at Sandy's farm," the boy said stubbornly.

Watching anger sweep darkly across Fraser's face, Lisa recalled her father saying he thought that Fraser was feeling the strain of being an only parent, and before he could threaten the child she said softly to Johnnie,

"Go with your daddy, Johnnie. He'll be all alone if you don't."

The boy gave her a puzzled glance, but went obediently and pushed his hand into Fraser's, turning to look back over his shoulder and call "Goodbye, Lisa."

She watched them go, her heart twisting painfully as she quelled an urge to go with them. It seemed more right and natural that she should be going with father and son, making three instead of two. But she was expected for tea and if she did not turn up everyone would wonder why she had not returned with Sandy.

As she walked across the field she wondered why Sarah

had deserted Fraser and had gone to tea with Sandy. Had she accepted Sandy's invitation in an attempt to pique Fraser? Was that why he had been so curt and hostile?

Certainly the model was on her best behaviour during tea, although occasionally on looking up Lisa surprised Sarah staring at her with something of the same hostility Fraser had shown, and she wondered what she had done to arouse such enmity. Nothing as far as she could tell except to get on too well with a little boy called Johnnie.

The thought bothered her for the rest of the evening and try as she might she could find no answer to the problem apart from leaving Ardmont altogether. Perhaps she should go with her father when he left? Perhaps if she went Johnnie would turn to Sarah, using her as a substitute for the friend he had lost?

But such answers did not please her. She did not want to leave Ardmont, and as it turned out she could not leave, nor could her father, because Aunt Maud had another severe stroke which left her paralysed all down one side making it necessary for her to have constant attention.

March was going out like a lion flinging a series of violent squalls at the village, tossing the tops of the trees, flattening the grass, snatching slates from roofs, tugging at the canvas covers of the yachts. Watching the wild weather from a window one day Lisa was sure the roof of the new shed down by the water would lift right off and fly away as she watched it ripple and pucker, only to have her view completely obscured suddenly by rain which hit the pane like a tropical torrent, sluicing down the glass noisily.

Later the same day she sat with Frank in the sitting room listening to a performance of Brahms' Fourth Symphony being broadcast from Glasgow by the Scottish National Orchestra. Leaning back in her chair, Lisa allowed herself to be swept along on a wave of romanticism caused by the bitter-sweet melodies.

Then through the sound of the music she became aware of an alien noise, the shrill burr-burr of the front door bell. She glanced at Frank. He had heard it too and stood up to turn down the volume of the radio. The bell sounded again.

"I'll answer," he said. "Whoever has come out on a night like this must be in need of help or slightly crazy."

He was back in a few minutes leading a small boy by the hand. It was Johnnie, his duffle coat open over his pyjamas, his feet bare, his blond hair dark with rain, his face streaked and blotched with crying.

"A young man to see you, Lisa," announced Frank quietly. "I think he's in trouble."

Lisa was out of her chair and kneeling before the child in an instant, propelled there by love and concern.

"Oh, Johnnie, what have you done?" she asked anxiously.

"I've run away from home," he muttered shakily, and promptly burst into tears.

It took a while for Lisa to pacify the sobbing child. When the flood of tears came to an end and he leaned against her, exhausted and shaken by sobs, she was able to push him on to the padded stool by the fire. Her father, who had left the room as soon as Johnnie had burst into tears, returned with a towel to dry the child's wet hair and a small tray bearing a glass of milk and some biscuits.

As he sipped the milk and munched biscuits some of Johnnie's composure came back and gradually Lisa was able to prise out of him his reason for running away from home.

"Have you been telling lies again and has your father been punishing you?" she asked gently.

"No." The expression in his big eyes was reproachful.

"Then why have you run away?"

"To punish him."

"Why? What has he done wrong?"

"He says he's going away again." He shuddered suddenly with sobs.

"To fetch another yacht?"

"I don't know. He says he'll be away more than a week."

"And you don't want him to go?"

"No. I hate him going away. I hate boats and sailing. I wish he did something else."

"But building boats and looking after them is your father's work," interposed Frank rather sternly. "He likes doing it. You can't expect him to change his work just because you don't like it. He has to earn his living and feed you and clothe you, and he's doing that in a way he knows best."

Johnnie turned to look at him, only half understanding this strange adult outlook.

"I . . . I wouldn't mind if I could go with him, but he says . . . he says . . ." here Johnnie gulped as tears welled again in his eyes, "he says I have to stay at home and go to school, and he'll get someone to look after me. I asked if he would ask you, Lisa, and he was very cross and said he wouldn't . . . and sent me to bed. So I ran away."

"You didn't run away far, young man," remarked Frank with a touch of dryness, and Johnnie gave him a timid glance and huddled closer to Lisa.

"Well, it was windy and wet, and I'm frightened of the wind," he defended weakly, "so I came to find Lisa."

"That was the right thing to do," she comforted, her thoughts straying to the man down at the white house behind the boatyard, whom Sandy had once described as being lonely and needing all the friends he could find. "But we'll have to tell your father that you're here. He'll be very upset in the morning if he looks in your bedroom and you aren't there."

She glanced at Frank, who nodded and slipped out of the room to use the telephone in the hall.

"He'll be very cross," whispered Johnnie. "He's been cross for days, ever since he came back on the big black boat. I don't think he likes me any more and wishes he didn't have me . . ."

"I'm sure he doesn't think anything like that," said Lisa with a confidence she was not feeling as she recalled her own suspicion that Johnnie's dislike of Sarah might be coming between the model and Fraser. "I expect he's worried about something and that's making him short-tempered."

Johnnie did not look in the least impressed by her suggestion, although he leaned his head against her shoulder and stared into the fire. They were unaware of the passage of time as they talked about the pictures they could see in the flames, and both of them turned rather guiltily when the door of the room swung open behind them and Fraser walked in. From the door Frank looked at Lisa and murmured, "I'll go and relieve Mrs. Ramsay. She's sat with Maud long enough tonight."

Fraser was breathing deeply as if he had run up the brae. Above the rolled neck of his dark sweater his face was pale and strained-looking and his eyes burned blue as he glanced briefly at Lisa before going to stand over Johnnie and ask abruptly,

"Why, Johnnie?"

"I didn't mean to stay away ... not for ever. I just wanted to frighten you," the boy blurted. Bursting into tears again, he flung himself at his father, clutching him round the thighs.

"Well, you succeeded," Fraser admitted with a grunt of laughter as he sat down on the stool and pulled his child between his knees. "But why?"

"Because you wouldn't ask Lisa to look after me while you're away. I won't mind you going if I can stay with her."

Over the boy's blond hair Fraser looked at Lisa, his eyes wary.

"You could have asked me, you know," she said softly. "Why didn't you?"

"You know damned well why," he grated between taut lips. Then the expression in his eyes softened as their gaze lingered almost hungrily on her face and once again she had that peculiar sensation as if he had touched her. "If you like, you can blame that abominable pride you once talked about," he added more gently, with the faintest glimmer of a smile.

Suddenly her legs felt weak and her head swam as if she were intoxicated. The confused feeling forced her to sit down in the nearest chair, and that was a mistake, because the stool he was sitting on was near to the chair and she found her face was on a level with his, too close for comfort so that she had to lean back.

"I suppose you didn't want to ask me because if I agreed you would be in my debt," she accused in a squeaky voice most unlike her own.

"Something like that," he drawled rather vaguely, looking away from her.

"Where are you going?"

"To a yacht-builders' conference in Essex, and then I was hoping to go over to Holland to visit a business associate."

"How long will you be away?" she asked, trying hard to be practical as he glanced at her again.

"About ten days."

"Don't you ever worry about Johnnie when you go away?" she queried. "Supposing you were in an accident, or were drowned when you're bringing a yacht here, don't you wonder what would happen to him without you?"

"Yes, I worry," he answered sharply, frowning. "More than you realise, perhaps."

"But not enough to stop you from going," she accused.

"He kicked up such a shindy this time that I'd more or less decided not to go, although it would mean losing contacts and probably contracts," he replied with a touch of impatience.

"Just because you couldn't swallow your pride and ask me to look after him," she scoffed gently.

He looked away from her again, his mouth tightening stubbornly. Johnnie, who had been resting quietly in his father's arms but who had been listening to every word, moved and muttered,

"Can I stay with Lisa, Daddy, while you go away?"

"That's for Lisa to decide," replied Fraser smoothly, pushing the boy away from him and rising to his feet. He picked up Johnnie's duffle coat from the floor and handed it to the boy. "Here, put this on and we'll go home," he ordered gruffly.

Lisa sighed and shivered. The moment of strange intimacy so shattering and revealing to herself was over. Fraser had

129

withdrawn behind his usual impassivity after having cleverly passed the buck to her, avoiding having to bend his stiff neck and ask her to mind his child.

"Very clever of you, Mr. Lamont," she jeered quietly, and saw the corner of his mouth quirk with amusement. "When would you want to leave Ardmont?"

"On Friday."

Lisa looked down at Johnnie's expectant face and knew she could not refuse the appeal in his eyes.

"Then when you come home from school on Friday afternoon, Johnnie, come straight here. I'll be waiting for you," she said, smiling at him.

Fraser stared at her with narrowed eyes.

"You're sure?" he asked. "Won't you have enough to do. I hear that Miss Roy is very poorly."

"My father is staying longer. He will help."

The straight line of his mouth relaxed as he caught Johnnie's upward hopeful glance.

"Well, son, it seems as if you've got what you wanted after all," he said lightly. "But you needn't be thinking that running away will always get this result. Shall we go home now?"

Johnnie's smile was evidence of his restored faith in human nature as he went with Fraser to the door.

"I've a feeling you've got what you wanted too, Mr. Lamont," drawled Lisa, unable to resist the temptation to provoke him as she followed them out into the hall.

Fraser swung round and gave her a level look which set her pulses leaping.

"Not quite," he replied. "My wants are more complex than Johnnie's and will take some time to achieve. Keep in touch with Jean Bridie. She'll know my movements next week and will let you know of any change of plan." He glanced down at his son's bare feet and finished, "You can't walk home like that."

He squatted down and Johnnie, apparently knowing what to do, climbed on to his back, twining his arms round his neck. Fraser put an arm under each of Johnnie's legs which were

130

spread across his back and shifted the child more securely on to his back, then stood up. Lisa opened the front door for them and lingered there after they had gone peering out into the stormy night. She thought she could hear Johnnie chuckling as his father ran with him down the road and she smiled to herself as she closed the door. Johnnie had got what he wanted, but his father's wants were more complex. She imagined they were like Romeo's:

> "More fierce and inexorable far
> Than empty tigers or the roaring sea."

But what were they?

She knew that one was the acquisition of more land to extend the boatyard. Was marriage to Sarah another? Either because he loved Sarah or because marriage to her would be advantageous in a way that his first marriage had not been. Sarah's parents were wealthy, well-connected, and would certainly would not cut her off if she married a Lamont, whose genealogy, while not aristocratic, was probably longer than that of a Chisholm.

Impatient with the direction her thoughts were taking, she went back into the sitting room. The empty glass and the scattered biscuit crumbs were the only signs that Johnnie had been there. But Fraser's presence seemed to linger, a bulky ghost in dark clothing with damp curling hair and blue-black eyes which occasionally looked at her as if they liked what they could see.

Too much imagination, that was her trouble, Lisa berated herself angrily as she knelt in front of the fire and picked up the poker to stir the glowing embers. She flung another log on the fire. It caught immediately and sparks flared up against the blackness of the chimney. Staring at them, Lisa was shaken suddenly by the memory of her own reaction to Fraser's physical presence in the room. Did such confusion mean she had fallen in love with him after all?

"Lisa?" Frank had come into the room, startling her. She jumped to her feet, feeling her heart pounding in her ears

"I think you'd better call Doctor Clarke. Aunt Maud has taken a turn for the worse."

Aunt Maud died on Friday morning just as the ferry taking Fraser to Gourock left the pier. Lisa was glad that Frank had stayed longer at Breck House because he was able to see to all the arrangements for the funeral, which was a simple affair held at the small church in the village and attended by all Maud Roy's friends and acquaintances, who gathered later at Breck House for refreshments. When they had all gone Lisa and Frank discussed Maud's will. Apart from a few small bequests to friends such as Mrs. Ramsay, she had left everything else including the house and a small annuity to Lisa on condition that the house was not sold during Lisa's lifetime and never to a Lamont. If Lisa attempted such a sale she would automatically forfeit both the house and the annuity, which would both be turned over to a charity.

"She really disliked the Lamont family, didn't she?" said Frank. "I wonder why?"

"I believe it had something to do with Fraser's grandfather, John Lamont. You know she was engaged to him at one time?"

"Yes, I knew, but I never knew the reason for her breaking off the engagement."

"Well, Mrs. Ramsay told me that someone in the village told Aunt Maud that John was seeing another young woman on the sly. She was furious and decided to confront him with the information. Apparently he was a very proud man and would neither deny nor admit that there was any truth in the story, so Aunt Maud broke off the engagement. A few years later he married someone else."

"So that's why she never married," said Frank. "Just as well, if she had so little faith. You know, I can't help thinking she's left you stuck with a white elephant. This house isn't exactly comfortable. Of course, you could always let the place to someone, I suppose, when you want to return to Manchester."

"But I'm not going to return to Manchester. I haven't any work to do there and I have here. Sandy has just received

132

orders for tweed suits designed by me, and then there's the sheepskin side of the business to be developed later this year. I'm staying here."

"Well, you must suit yourself, of course," said Frank mildly, giving her a shrewd assessing glance. "But the cost of upkeep on a place like this will be considerable. I doubt if the annuity will cover it."

"Then I'll take in lodgers in the summer. Bed and break-fast," she said.

"Yes, I can imagine the advertisement," he answered with a laugh. "Come and stay at Breck House, plumbing suspect, draughts considerable, wonderful view of boatyard. Well, I think I'll love and leave you for a while and depart for London and warmer climates. I'll let you know where I'll be going after my leave is over. I'm hoping for a position in Whitehall. Time I settled down."

Frank left on Wednesday's boat and after seeing him off Lisa walked slowly back along the pier. The day was warm and sunny. In the gardens of the staid Victorian villas, clumps of daffodils and narcissi nodded in the faint breeze. April was in, that most tender and cruel of months when desire leapt in the blood and memory stirred painfully. Not the best time of the year to die, Johnnie had said when she had told him about Aunt Maud, and now, looking around her, she could not help but agree with him, because today Ardmont, the kyle, the distant mountains and islands all looked their best. Colours were deep and clear, sharply delineated. The sea was indigo blue speckled with white-crested waves, edged by the pale curves of sandy beaches above which emerald and ochre fields were crowned by bottle green woodland which gave way to bracken brown moors and pale mauve rock. It was days like this, coming after the periods of interminable storm-grey, that made Lisa realise why Aunt Maud and others had stayed to live in this remote peninsula, made her understand why Fraser had returned, for here there was peace and unspoiled beauty.

At the mill she found Ina in one of her tizzies. The April

version of two of the magazines carried advertisements of Ardmont tweeds showing Sarah slim and elegant wearing the suits designed by Lisa, and already Sandy had received several telephone enquiries.

"Och, I'm so excited I could do a jig!" exclaimed Ina, who was already capering round the office, much to Sandy's amusement.

"I'm beginning to wonder how we're going to meet any orders we might receive. You can't possibly make all the articles of clothing, Ina," he said. "You'll need help. Do you know of anyone who would come and work here under your supervision?"

"Not off-hand. But I'll make some enquiries amongst me friends in Glasgow."

"I'll have to hire someone extra to work in the office too, to answer written enquiries and to organise the mailing of brochures and goods," continued Sandy with an air of suppressed excitement after Ina had left the room. "And all thanks to you, Lisa. You'll have to become a partner now. I can't afford to let you go."

"Well, I'm not thinking of going anywhere. I'm staying in Ardmont. You've only to ask me, Sandy, and I'll do more designs," she replied.

"But you must be paid. If you won't join the company we'll have to arrange something else on a commission basis. Supposing I think about it, discuss it with Mother and Dad who are the other directors of the company and then see you one evening next week? It's so difficult to discuss anything here with the noise of the machinery and people coming and going all the time. If you'd come up to the farm one evening . . ."

"That isn't possible. You forget I'm looking after Johnnie and he goes to bed at seven. Why don't you come to Breck House instead?"

He frowned and looked rather dubious.

"Well, I suppose it will be all right. I wouldn't like anyone to think . . ." he began diffidently.

"Oh, come off it, Sandy. You wouldn't have hesitated to

come if Aunt Maud had been there upstairs in bed."

"No, I wouldn't. But it's different now. You're alone and a.."

"Listen, these days a man can go calling on a girl who lives alone without anyone thinking wrong things. Why, in Manchester . . . or any city . . ."

"Yes, in the city, but not here, Lisa. The people here are still very conventional in outlook," he objected seriously.

"Sandy, if I were a man and you wanted to do business with me would you hesitate to call on me in the evening?" she challenged.

"No, I wouldn't," he admitted.

"Then will you please forget my sex and treat me as an equal if you want me to design for you?"

"I'm not sure that I can," he said slowly, staring at her with puzzled eyes.

"Try," she urged. "Or otherwise I can't join your company."

CHAPTER VII

LISA spent the week-end gardening and walking with Johnnie. He was good company and she realised that when he returned to his own home Breck House would seem empty and lonely. There would be no Aunt Maud to talk to or listen to. Although she had not lived with her for very long Lisa missed the old lady's caustic comments and often found herself staring at the big wing chair, placed in the window of the sitting room and in which her aunt had liked to sit, with a feeling of sad regret, wishing that she had come to Ardmont more often to visit her.

But she would not feel lonely for long, she vowed to herself. Being alone was part of being independent, of being free. She had plenty of inner resources to fall back on so that she need never feel lonely. Aunt Maud, herself independent and heartwhole, had made it possible for her to be independent. She was free in the full sense of the word; free to develop her potentialities as a designer and as a woman.

As a woman? Her thoughts stumbled over the phrase. How could she in all honesty say that she could develop fully as a woman on her own? How could she fulfil her destiny as a woman without the love of a man? Deliberately she willed herself not to think such treacherous thoughts, conveniently ignoring the fact that she had lain awake several nights since Fraser had left Ardmont, wondering where he was and what he was doing, imagining what their next meeting would be like and wishing that were not so many barriers between her and him.

Sandy came on Tuesday evening just as a sliver of a new moon appeared over the hump of Boag, silvering the small clouds which drifted near it and winking at itself in the pallid water of the kyle. He stayed not more than an hour and all the time he seemed ill at ease. But at the end of that time Lisa had consented to become a partner in Ardmont Tweeds Limited and also to be chief designer.

Sandy spoke of nothing else but business and Lisa decided that this was the "important thing" about which he had always wanted to tell her and was relieved. When the clock struck nine he rose promptly and said he must be on his way. Lisa went with him to the front door and they stood together on the doorstep for a few minutes admiring the sheen of moonlight on the sleek water and talking in a desultory fashion about the future of the mill.

Then with a suddenness which took her completely by surprise Sandy bent and kissed her on the lips. It was a brief kiss, shy and feather-like, but it left her in no doubt that he would have liked to have made it longer and more demanding if he had considered it the time and place.

"To seal a bargain which I hope neither of us will ever regret in the hopes that it will lead to a more binding relationship," he whispered. "Goodnight, Lisa."

He went quickly along the path and her amazed farewell was said to his back. The gate clanged after him and she heard the granite chips of the roadway crunching beneath his quick feet as he went down the brae.

"Very interesting," observed a masculine voice through which a tantalising thread of laughter ran, and she whirled round. Fraser was standing only a few feet away from her, the crisp crest of his hair and the clear-cut angles of his face easily discernible in the moonlight.

"What are you doing here?" she demanded, thoroughly confused by the sight of him.

"I came to call on you and to offer my condolences, having only just heard of Miss Roy's death. I was about to press the doorbell when the door started to open and I heard you and Sandy talking. I ducked to one side and was treated to the sight of him giving you a goodnight kiss. Almost as good as going to the cinema," he scoffed.

"He was sealing a bargain," she retorted. "I have agreed to become a partner in Ardmont Tweeds."

"First time I've seen one business partner kiss another one," he mocked.

"I didn't expect you until tomorrow," she said, deciding to ignore his jibes.

"Sarah drove me down from Glasgow. She left me at the bottom of the brae. It's a pity we weren't a little later, then she could have given Sandy a lift home," he said dryly.

"Oh, so you've been with her after all," she accused.

"I'm not quite sure how to take that," he drawled, coming closer. "What do you mean by saying I've been with her, in that tone of voice?"

"Someone told me that she was away too in the south of England and on the Continent, and I thought . . ."

"Not very nice thoughts," he interrupted sharply, and she felt as if he had rapped her on the knuckles. "No, I have not been with Sarah for the last ten days. I met her at Abbotsinch Airport this evening and she offered to drive me down here, so I accepted. It was she who told me about Miss Roy. I'm sorry. You must miss her."

"Yes, I do."

There was silence between them. It was so quiet Lisa could hear the distant swish of waves on the shore and the quacking of nesting ducks amongst the reeds on the islands. She kept her eyes on the shimmering path of moonlight. She was afraid to look at Fraser when she knew he was looking at her.

"Last time I returned home you invited me to breakfast," he murmured. "I hope that this time you might invite me in for some supper. There wasn't time to eat on the way here. Also I have something to ask you and I would rather ask it behind closed doors."

"I expect it could keep until tomorrow."

It had been one thing inviting Sandy into the house, but it was quite another to invite Fraser while he had such a peculiar effect on her senses.

"I expect it could, but my appetite can't," he replied. "There's nothing to eat in the cupboard at my house. Would you have me go to bed hungry?"

He was beguiling her, using his voice, his physical nearness, his knowledge of the purely feminine instinct to provide food for the homecomer to get his own way. The change in his approach disconcerted her and she found it impossible to refuse.

"Come in," she invited, and turned into the house.

In the kitchen she found cheese and crackers. Wondering what to offer him to drink, she came across a bottle of beer left by her father. She placed it with an opener and a glass tankard in front of Fraser, who was already sitting at the table and helping himself to the cheese. He gave her a grateful glance and she noticed that now she could see him properly he looked weary. Dark lines were scored under his eyes and his face looked thinner. Whatever had caused the strain before he had left Ardmont had not been lifted by his trip to Essex and Holland.

"What do you want to ask me about?" she asked, watching him pour beer into the tankard. When the bottle was half empty he stopped pouring to offer her some.

Discovering that her throat was dry, she nodded and fetched a glass for herself, then held it out for him to pour the rest of the beer into it. Then she sat down at the table and helped herself to a piece of the Dunlop cheese and began to nibble it, thinking how much more natural it seemed to be sitting here in the kitchen with Fraser than it had been to sit with Sandy in the sitting room.

"I want to ask you about this house," said Fraser. "Who owns it now?"

"I do. You knew Aunt Maud was going to leave it to me."

"That was what she said to stop me from asking her to sell it to me. It didn't have to be true," he replied cynically.

"Well, it was," she replied shortly, bracing herself for the question she guessed would come next.

"Will you sell it and the land to me?" he asked curtly.

"No. And even if I wanted to I couldn't."

"Why not?"

"By the terms of the will I can't sell it, and certainly not to a Lamont."

His eyes narrowed unpleasantly and she had an awful feeling he was going to say something nasty about Aunt Maud. But he didn't. Instead he finished his beer and then attacked the cheese again.

"I see," he said slowly. "Can *you* build on the land?"

"I don't know. It didn't occur to me to ask the lawyer."

He ate more cheese and judging by the frown on his face he was thinking hard. Gradually the frown faded and when he spoke it was to ask casually,

"Has Johnnie been good?"

Relieved that he had decided to leave the subject of Breck House, Lisa launched into an account of Johnnie's behaviour and doings.

"He seems to have had a good time," commented Fraser. "And so do you. It's a relief to hear that he didn't have one tantrum or keep you up several nights on the run."

"He would only do that if he felt insecure. Every time you go away you upset his very precarious sense of security, because you've always been the one stable person in his life. If he had a mother he would react to your absences quite differently because she would provide the security and the stability too. Even the same baby-sitter would be able to do that. But you've used so many different people," said Lisa forthrightly.

"Do you think I don't know that?" he snapped. "I've tried in many ways to be both mother and father to him, but having a business to run makes it difficult. And then he either takes a violent dislike to a baby-sitter, or they take a dislike to him or to me . . . I'm not sure which. Short of not going away at all I can't think of any way out of the problem, and if I don't go away occasionally the business will suffer."

"You could marry again," said Lisa quietly.

"Who would I marry?" he said with a touch of bitterness. "It has to be someone Johnnie likes or otherwise I would just be creating a hell for three people."

He stared broodingly at the empty tankard, and Lisa's mind flicked to Sarah. He must want to marry the beautiful model, as she had guessed, but Johnnie was in the way.

"Wouldn't you have to love her too?" she queried.

"Respect would be all that was necessary," he replied coldly, "and she wouldn't have to mind when I wanted to go away on my own."

Slightly chilled by his answer which made it clear that he would consider a marriage of convenience for Johnnie's sake, Lisa sharpened her claws for an argument on the relative rights of women and men.

"Would you mind if she went off on her own occasionally and was independent?"

"Not at all. I would welcome such an attitude. It would make me feel easier in my mind. I value my own personal freedom so much that I'd hate to be responsible for curbing another's. I couldn't stand the sort of woman who would cling and weep every time I wanted to go away. It's that more than anything else which has put me off marrying again."

Had Holly clung and wept? wondered Lisa. She was suddenly sorry for the pale ghost of the girl who had been pretty and gay and just a little timid and who had possibly bruised herself against Fraser's rock-like hardness.

"Not all women cling and weep," she retorted.

He cocked a satirical eyebrow at her and then grinned,

"Meaning that you don't, I suppose," he said, leaning back in his chair. He stretched his legs under the table and folded his arms across his chest and looked at her in that slow considering way which always made her skin tingle.

"You know, when I think about it, you'd suit very well," he drawled. "Johnnie likes you and you like him. You're sufficiently independent not to make any demands which I couldn't meet, you wouldn't cling and weep. In fact, if I wasn't aware that marriage is low on your list of priorities I would ask you now to marry me for Johnnie's sake."

It seemed to Lisa that all the blood drained back to her heart, making it over-full, ready to burst. Her face white, her eyes dark pools of greenish light between long dark lashes, her hair a burnished red helmet beneath the glare of the electric light, she faced him across the table, wishing that there was some way in which she could throw his challenge back in his face. It would serve him right if she took it up, she thought furiously.

Aloud she said: "You mean a marriage of convenience?"

"All marriages are convenient in some way or other," he replied smoothly. "This one would be convenient for Johnnie and provide him with a mother he would like to have."

"And how would it be convenient for you?" she asked in her coolest voice, although her eyes were blazing with anger.

"I wouldn't have to worry about him while I was away, that's all."

"And how would it be convenient for me?" she asked finally.

"That would be for you to decide, of course," he replied, and stood up. "But it's merely a passing thought I had, because I know you have every intention of remaining unmarried, that being the fashionable thing for women to do these days, apparently."

Lisa's reaction was impulsive and irrational. Aware only of an overwhelming urge to surprise him, to shake him out of his bland assumptions about herself, she rose to her feet, swept round the table to stand before him, her head held high.

"On the contrary, Mr. Lamont," she said coolly, looking him straight in the eyes, "for Johnnie's sake even I would give up my single status. You're on."

"What do you mean?" The sharpness of his voice and the widening of his eyes gave her a fleeting moment of pleasure and triumph. She had called his bluff and for once he was disconcerted.

"I mean that you can go ahead and ask me to marry you and I'll accept your proposal. You see, just lately I've changed the order of my priorities. You've made your suggestion at the time when marriage is first on the list."

He stared at her in silence, but it was impossible to assess

142

his feelings because now he had himself well under control.

Then he began to laugh, quiet laughter which sent alarm flickering along Lisa's nerves. It was as if he was laughing at a joke he had no intention of sharing with her, and she had a suspicion the joke was on her.

"Well, that's a change in attitude," he scoffed.

"No more of a change than in yours," she retorted. "I seem to remember that at one time you had no use for women who made friends with your son."

"That was before I realised that he liked you and that your liking for him had nothing to do with me," he replied more seriously. Then giving her a sharp underbrowed glance he added more crisply, "All right. I'm asking you to marry me, Red Smith, the sooner the better for Johnnie's sake, because I have to go away again at the beginning of May to bring a yacht over from Ireland. Would May the first suit you, before the Registrar? It isn't long since Miss Roy died, so I'm sure you won't want a church ceremony with all the trimmings, and I'd prefer a quiet quick affair myself because I'll have to go away the same day."

Vaguely, as if in a dream, Lisa found herself agreeing while she smothered an image of herself floating down the aisle of the village church in a white dress which she had designed herself. Within minutes she was standing on the front door step exactly where she had stood with Sandy only an hour previously. The moonlit night was mild, the air heavy with the scent of lilac. Ducks still quacked amongst the reeds and in the distance a dog barked.

"A night for bargains to be struck and sealed," said Fraser derisively. "I'd seal ours, but that would be making an unnecessary demand on you. I'd like to see Johnnie before he goes to school tomorrow. Will you send him down, please?"

Lisa wondered why she should feel so disappointed because he had decided not to seal their bargain in the same way that Sandy had.

"No, you come to breakfast instead," she invited impulsively.

He looked at her, and smiled. It might have been a trick of the moonlight but it seemed to her that his smile had a faintly wicked triumphant quality.

"You're on," he said, and turned away to walk down the path.

In the night Lisa remembered that smile of Fraser's. He had looked, she decided, as if he had won a victory. It was at that point that she got out of bed and opened the door of her room determined to go downstairs and phone him even though it was two o'clock in the morning, and tell him that she had changed her mind again, that she was not prepared to marry him for anyone's sake. But she had not gone downstairs. Instead she had paced the bedroom, pausing now and then to stare out at the sky darkening above the island as the moon slowly slid out of sight.

Why had she suddenly ditched all her dearly held principles about love and marriage and had agreed to marry Fraser Lamont for convenience? Convenience to whom? To Johnnie and him. But what was there convenient about such a marriage for her? Nothing, as far as she could see. And yet the decision to marry had been hers. Why?

Because, with all his talk of how she fitted the bill exactly for the position of Johnnie's stepmother, Fraser had dangled a tempting bait before her and she had risen, as he had known she would.

Lisa cringed and squirmed in bed as she realised how easily and readily she had risen while her will had been in abeyance.

She could not go through with it. Now that she had recovered her wits, she realised it. She could not have people like Sarah Popham pointing at her in scorn, and she would tell Fraser so when she saw him at breakfast.

In the kitchen as she prepared the meal she went over all she would say to him. She would tell him that he did not have to marry her if he wanted her to look after Johnnie. She would do that any time he asked.

Johnnie was already downstairs in the dining room playing

Aunt Maud's old tinkling piano – or at least pretending he could play it. The front door bell rang and she heard him scamper through the hall to answer it, his shriek of delight when he saw his father, and her heart started to pound. Nothing would make her go out into the hall to greet Fraser. He could find his own way to the kitchen.

It was a while before he appeared and she had just finished frying eggs when the kitchen door burst open and Johnnie rushed in and flung his arms round the top of her legs.

"Lisa, Daddy says you're going to be my mummy. Is it true?" he demanded.

She looked across the room at Fraser, who stood just inside the door watching her narrowly. No sleepless night for him, she thought, noting that the lines of weariness and strain had gone from his face.

"Lisa, it is true, isn't it?" whispered Johnnie urgently. Looking down at him, she could see doubt and disappointment dawning in his wide eyes.

"If your father says so it must be true, mustn't it?" she replied, rather uncertainly.

"Oh, goodie!" Johnnie danced round the room. "Wait till I tell Jim that I'm going to have a real mummy like him!"

"Johnnie," cautioned Lisa, flinging an exasperated glance at Fraser, "I don't think you should tell anyone just yet."

But Johnnie was deaf to her remark.

"And Miss Hargraves, my teacher, will be pleased," he continued gaily. "She's always saying I look as if I need a mother to look after me."

At this rate the whole village, the whole peninsula would know by noon, thought Lisa helplessly, and glared at Fraser as he took his place at the table.

"Devil!" she mouthed silently at him, remembering rather belatedly Aunt Maud's warnings about him, and he had the insolence to laugh openly at her as Johnnie rattled on about the numerous people who would be pleased when he told them that he was going to have a mother.

"Would Miss Roy have been pleased too?" he asked suddenly, and Lisa thought how horrified Aunt Maud would have been to learn that her only surviving relative, on whom she had depended to keep Breck House out of the hands of the Lamont family, had agreed to marry a Lamont.

Again she glared at Fraser and received an amused glance in return.

"Of course she would," he said smoothly to Johnnie. "When she was younger she wanted to marry your great-grandfather."

"Why didn't she?" asked the boy.

"He decided to marry someone else," replied Fraser easily, and Johnnie was silent as he tried to work out this new puzzle.

"Do you know where Frank is?" Fraser asked Lisa.

It took her some time to realise he was referring to her father.

"Yes, I do. I had a letter from him yesterday. He's staying with some friends on the Riviera."

"Then I'd like to suggest that you send him a cable asking his opinion and possibly his permission before we inform the Registrar."

She was surprised. His whole approach to the matter had been so unconventional so far that she had not expected him to even think her father had any say. She was just about to declare that she didn't need Frank's permission to marry when she remembered suddenly that Fraser had married Holly against her parents' wishes and had regretted his action. So she said meekly,

"Yes, I will."

It would help, she decided, to have her father's opinion and would give her some much needed breathing space before the notice of the forthcoming marriage was posted in the window of the registrar's office in the nearby market town of Kilbride. But as she telephoned the cable she wondered who was listening on the local switchboard. How right Fraser had been when he had once told her nothing could be done in Ardmont without the whole place knowing about it!

As soon as she could she went to the mill to tell Sandy before he heard the news from the grapevine. To describe him as being surprised was to underestimate his reaction. He was flabbergasted and sat for a while, silent and staring. Then he stood up and went to look out of the office window to hide the expression on his face.

"I can scarcely believe it," he croaked at last. "You said nothing of this last night."

"I didn't know, because he hadn't asked me. He came to see me after you'd gone."

"But you must have had some inkling, some idea of what was in his mind? A man doesn't suddenly propose marriage. He has to lead up to it in various ways."

Lisa was silent. How could she explain to Sandy or even expect him to understand Fraser's mocking challenge and her own reaction when she hardly understood them herself?

"Would it have made any difference to your offer of a partnership to me if you'd thought I was going to be married?" she asked.

He came back to the desk and looked down at her.

"Of course it would. You must see that, Lisa. As a married woman your loyalties will be, must be, to your husband first. Any business commitments will come afterwards."

"I don't see it that way," she argued stubbornly.

"What about Fraser? What does he think? Supposing I want you to go away on business for the company, what would he say then?"

"He would let me go, just as I would let him go. I wouldn't have agreed to marry him if I hadn't known he would let me do what he does himself."

Sandy looked thoroughly puzzled. "Sounds more like a business partnership than marriage," he said.

"But don't you see, that's what marriage should be; a partnership between equals," replied Lisa, slightly astounded to realise she was defending her future relationship with Fraser.

Sandy rubbed a hand across his head, making his fine reddish hair stand up spikily.

"No, I'm afraid I don't see. Marriage for me is loving and caring for someone."

"And as long as she loves and cares for you and keeps her place in the home and cooks your meals and washes your clothes and is there when you come home from work you're prepared to go on loving and caring for her," said Lisa tartly. Then seeing a rather sad, disillusioned expression cross his face she blurted, "Oh, I'm sorry, Sandy. It's obvious your ideas and mine on this particular subject don't coincide. I couldn't be that sort of wife. I . . . I'm too wild a bird to be happy caged."

"Yes, I can see that now," he said with a touch of dryness, his eyes suddenly very clear. "I hope you'll be happy, Lisa. I'm sure that in choosing you Fraser has done the best for his boy. I know you're fond of the child and that he responds to you. It's just that it happened so suddenly, when I'd thought Fraser was looking in Sarah's direction and she was hoping . . ."

Lisa didn't hear the rest of his sentence because a flash of light flickered through her mind like lightning, illuminating a good reason for accepting Fraser's proposal. Once Sarah knew Fraser was marrying herself, she was bound to turn elsewhere, and why shouldn't the model turn to Sandy, who had waited all these years?

"Now it's your turn to hope," she said softly.

"Perhaps," he replied rather heavily. "Now, about these new enquiries for tweed suits, I was thinking we should make up some samples of the tweeds available to send out to prospective buyers."

Lisa turned her attention to business, knowing that in some way she had hurt him, and it was not until she saw Ina later that she learned how.

"I must say ye're a sly one," teased Ina, having already heard the news somehow about the forthcoming marriage. "Ye never let on even when I talked about Sarah having it in for ye. Now I know why she did. When's the wedding to be?"

"Soon. Probably the first of May."

"Och, the man's in a hurry and no mistake!"

"It's for Johnnie's sake. He needs a mother," said Lisa defensively, and wondering how many times in the next few weeks she would be trotting out that reason.

"Aye, I can see that, but there must be a bit more to it than that," said Ina, with a knowing twinkle in her eyes. Then as she saw no answering humour in Lisa's eyes her ripe red mouth made a round shape of surprise. "Ye're never telling me that you and he are marrying for convenience?"

"Yes, I am. There's nothing wrong in that, is there?"

"Well, I'll be blowed!" Now the shape of Ina's eyes matched the shape her mouth had made. Her face sobering, she jerked her head in the direction of Sandy's office. "The boss isn't any too pleased. He's been walking around all morning with a face like a wet week. I canna' help feeling a wee bit sorry for him, especially after what ye've just told me."

"Why should he be miserable? I've told him I'm still willing to be a partner in the company," replied Lisa, with a touch of impatience.

Ina shook her head slowly as if she considered Lisa less intelligent than she had thought.

"I've never met a lass like ye, so sophisticated on the outside and so innocent underneath. It's not that which is upsetting him. Have ye not noticed he has a fancy for ye himself, and now by promising to marry yon Lamont ye've dashed all his hopes?"

"But he loves Sarah . . . or used to do."

Again Ina shook her head.

"Not since you came to Ardmont, he hasn't. Och, the poor lad! It's more than a body can take . . . to love and not be loved in return twice in his life," she said with a sniff and a glint of tears in her eyes.

It was no use her thinking she was helping Sandy by marrying Fraser, thought Lisa ruefully, as she walked the dogs later that afternoon. What she had tried to avoid had happened. He had been in the process of falling in love with her ever since she had stepped ashore with him last December, she realised, as she cast her mind back over their friendship. The invitations to tea at the farm, to go walking when it was fine, the number of times he found excuses to talk to her in his office at the mill, his wanting her to be a partner in the company — they had all been part of his slow, shy approach and had culminated in the kiss he had given her last night to seal a bargain which he had hoped would lead to a more binding relationship.

She should have known that a man like Sandy, extremely conventional and slightly old-fashioned in his attitude to women, would never had made such approaches if he had not wanted more from her than she was prepared to give. But having been brought up to be natural and at ease with the opposite sex and to regard herself as any man's equal she had not realised that he would read into her naturalness with him a depth of liking for him which had led him to hope for more.

"Cooee, Lisa!" Johnnie's voice was shrill and carried on the still soft afternoon air.

She looked round. He was chugging along the road behind her, coat flapping, hair flying. When he reached her he smiled up at her and asked breathlessly,

"Are you still going to be my mummy?"

"I . . . I think so."

"Goodie! I was afraid you might have changed your mind."

Remembering how close she had been to changing her mind that morning Lisa blushed rather guiltily, and he noticed. His smile faded and he looked reproachful.

"You . . . you wouldn't change your mind, would you, Lisa?" he whispered.

"No, I wouldn't do that."

"Cross your heart and hope to die?" This was something he had learned recently from Jim.

"Cross my heart," she repeated.

She was caught, she thought, caught in a trap of her own making; caught by an affection-starved child who looked up at her with his father's eyes. And although, like a wild bird, she had made several attempts to be free of this trap, they had not been very vigorous or determined attempts.

"Are you coming to make our supper tonight?" asked Johnnie.

"No, I'm not."

"But you should if you're going to be my mummy."

"No. Not until I'm living with you, and not always then. Your father is a very good cook."

"But mummies always make the supper. Jim's does," he wailed.

Lisa realised that this was something she must get straight before she went any further.

"Just because I'm going to be your mummy doesn't mean I have to do everything Jim's mummy does. I expect I'll get your meals lots of times and I'll always be there when your daddy isn't. But sometimes I won't be there, and then your daddy will look after you as he does now. Do you understand?"

He stared at her solemnly before he nodded his head.

"As long as you're there most of the time. I don't want you to be like Jim's mummy. She's fat and she hasn't got eyes the colour of mountain pools when the sun shines on them . . ."

"Like what?" Lisa interrupted, astounded by this flow of words.

He squirmed a little and then repeated what he had said, adding defensively,

"That's what Daddy said they were like when I asked him what colour your eyes are 'cos I didn't know. He said they were green and brown like the pools in the mountains where he goes fishing sometimes. And he said your hair is the colour of the leaves of the copper beech tree in the garden at Creddon Hall. Lisa, don't you like what he said?"

"Yes, yes." She found she was shaky and breathless. "Yes, of course I do."

The likening of the colour of her hair to the leaves of the copper beech tree was very different from the scornful "Red" which Fraser had once used and which he persisted in calling her, and hearing his opinion of her colouring second-hand

151

from his son gave her an odd feeling of having eavesdropped on his most private thoughts; thoughts which she would never have suspected him of having.

Possessing this new knowledge of her future husband made her look forward to seeing him again. She expected him to come to Breck House to discuss the arrangements for their marriage in more detail, but he did not come and she did not see him for two days. Remembering rather belatedly that it was to be a marriage of convenience in which the usual rules of courtship did not apply, she realised eventually that he would not call to her to see her unless it was absolutely necessary.

Consequently she started to look for excuses to go to the boatyard to see him and found a very useful one in the arrival of a cable from her father in answer to the one she had sent him. Frank had been brief and explicit.

"Delighted by your news. Proceed with my blessing."

His reply surprised Lisa. Frank was not the sort of person who went in for transports of delight, being very reserved when it came to expressing his emotions. She had realised that during his stay in Ardmont he had formed a good opinion of Fraser, but she had not thought he had known him long enough to consider him seriously as a prospective son-in-law.

The day was damp and grey, and down in the boatyard an aggravating little wind whipped round the corners of the big sheds, blowing the wood-shavings and pieces of cardboard about and snatching at the canvas coverings of the yachts. From the sound of one shed came the noise of an electrical saw and peering into the shed Lisa's attention was caught by the beautiful workmanship and rakish lines of the yacht being built in there, and she stood for a moment rapt in admiration for the smooth planking of red-gold mahogany curving from bow to stern.

On the slip another yacht was ready to be launched. It also possessed the fine lines of the one in the shed but it gleamed with new paint and on its bow its name glittered in gold-incised lettering: MADRIGAL.

Fraser stood near its high bow, in characteristic pose, hands on his hips, head tilted slightly back as he watched the boat slip gradually backwards into the grey wind-flurried water. Then it was afloat, swinging on the current, looking slightly ill at ease until its engine started up and one of the men on board took the wheel and steered the stately yacht away from the slip towards the black mooring buoy which bobbed a few yards away from the slip.

"I like her lines," said Lisa. "Who owns her?"

Fraser turned sharply to look at her, not having heard her approach.

"She belongs to Ranald Gow, Harry Chisholm's brother-in-law," he replied brusquely.

Meeting his eyes suddenly, Lisa remembered his description of hers. If hers were like mountain pools in the sunlight his were like the sea on one of those perfect days of sun and wind, deep indigo, mysterious and yet somehow inviting.

She blinked quickly, conscious that she was turning pink and that he looked faintly amused.

"Do you want to see me about something? If so would you mind being quick? We have two more yachts to launch."

"Isn't it a bad day for launching?" she stuttered, wanting to show an interest in his work about which she knew so little. "I mean, the wind must be a nuisance."

"It isn't perfect, but it will do, and at this time of the year, with so many owners demanding that their yachts be ready by the end of April or even before, we can't afford to waste time," he explained patiently. "Now, what can I do for you?"

She held out the cable, telling herself she must not be hurt by his brusqueness and apparent lack of pleasure on seeing her. Theirs was a business arrangement and there would be no room for being hurt or taking offence. If he was busy she must state what she wanted and get out of his way quickly. But she could not help wishing he had smiled at her.

He handed the cable back to her after reading it.

"Well, that puts us in the clear with regard to your father. Kind of him to be quick in replying. Now we can go ahead and inform the registrar. We have three clear weeks before the first of May, which is all that is required." He slanted a derisive glance at her. "Know of anyone who might object?"

"No one. If my father had been against it would you have backed out?" she challenged.

"Would you?" he countered.

"That isn't a proper answer."

"It's all you're getting now. Think you could give Johnnie his supper tonight? I'd like to stay down here until these boats are in the water."

"Would you like me to put him to bed too?" she queried with mock meekness.

"It would help," he replied curtly, and walked off into one of the sheds.

Johnnie was very pleased to have Lisa prepare his supper. He insisted on having it in his own home and so Lisa went there reluctantly. Once inside the house she was rather appalled to see the state it was in. The living room was thick with dust, and books and newspapers were scattered everywhere. The dining room, a dim dusty room, looked as if no one had entered it for years. In the kitchen dirty breakfast dishes were still on the table. The whole ground floor of the house looked dismal and uninviting on that grey April day.

She stood in the middle of the kitchen wondering where to start. She could not possibly prepare and serve a meal in such conditions.

"It's worse upstairs," volunteered Johnnie, who was watching the play of expression on her face.

"Worse? It couldn't be. Hasn't Mrs. Wilson been to clean this week?"

He shook his head solemnly. "Mrs. Wilson is ill, so she can't come, and Daddy's been too busy to bother with housework."

Slowly Lisa took off her coat.

"Then you and I are going to work very hard for the next two hours, Johnnie Lamont," she announced.

Later, as the light died slowly in the western sky, Lisa finished reading a story to Johnnie, tucked him into his bed, kissed him good night and went downstairs, thinking back to that night in January when he had wanted her to stay for supper and she had longed to stay and see him to bed. Well, her wish had come true in a very unexpected way.

Downstairs in the living room she flopped into a deep armchair and yawned. Never had she felt so tired. Since she had entered the house almost four hours ago she had washed dishes, scrubbed the kitchen floor, changed the sheets on two beds, and, grateful because Fraser had had the sense to install an automatic washing machine, she had loaded it with all the dirty clothes she could find. She had cleaned the bathroom, vacuumed as much as she had time for, had prepared a meal and eaten it with Johnnie, made him have a bath and had seen him to bed.

In all that time Fraser had not put in an appearance at the house. Occasionally glancing out of the window, she had seen him crossing the yard and had noticed at least one other yacht take to the water. She assumed that he would stay down there until the third one was safely launched and moored for the night. He would be like that, she thought sleepily, working right through until a job was finished before he relaxed and came home to eat.

Now she knew why she had rebelled for so long against the idea of marriage. No woman used to freedom and independence as she was could do the sort of work she had just done willingly. Only for love would a woman submit willingly to such slavery. Only for love ... Her head dropped against the hard stuffed back of the armchair and she slept.

She was on a sailing boat for the first time in her life. It skimmed over indigo blue water, its sails like white wings spread out from the mast. She lay on the foredeck watching the ripple of the bow wave, happier than she had ever felt in her life. Then from behind her Fraser's voice barked an order. She obeyed immediately. More orders came, fast and furious, sending her scurrying from one side of the boat to the other, until she was breathless, bruised and bleeding. The orders stopped and she turned hopefully, expecting a reward. But he wasn't looking at her. Beside him sat Sarah, laughing up at him, and while Lisa stood transfixed he bent his head and kissed Sarah . . .

Lisa opened her eyes. A shiver ran through her body. She was crouched in the armchair in the dark room and she felt cold. Uncurling herself stiffly, she stood up and shook her head to clear it of the stupid but vivid dream.

The front door opened.

"Fraser? Are you there?"

That was Sarah's voice calling. Running her fingers through her hair, Lisa went out into the hall and switched on the light. She could see Sarah standing outside the door.

"No, he isn't here yet, Sarah," she called. "Won't you come in?"

Sarah came in. She was as immaculate as ever and her mouth was as tempting and provocative as it had been in the dream.

"Since you ask me, yes, I'll come in and wait for him," she drawled, and the ice in her voice put Lisa on her guard. "I've a few things I want to say to you."

They went into the living room, but neither of them sat down. They stood eyeing each other like two cats about to start a fight.

"I've just been talking to Sandy," said Sarah. "He's not happy about this arrangement between you and Fraser. It was the first I'd heard about it because I've been busy helping Mother entertain some guests. Is it true? Are you and Fraser going to be married?"

"Yes, it's true."

"So I was right after all! You're no better than those other women who made friends with Johnnie, with an eye to the future. Only you were more clever as well as being attractive in an unusual way. You pretended you weren't interested in marriage. And of course the fact that the child likes you must have weighed heavily in your favour. Still, I'm not as con-

156

vinced as Sandy is that Fraser is marrying you for Johnnie's sake. I think he has a much more ingenious and subtle reason."

Lisa, who had been congratulating herself on her self-control in the face of Sarah's spiteful insults, looked up sharply.

"Oh? What is that?" she asked.

Sarah's lovely eyes narrowed cunningly and then their gaze slid away, avoiding Lisa's direct glance. With her hip-swinging walk she swayed up and down the room a couple of times before she answered.

"The annoying thing is I think I might have put the idea into his head," she said at last, coming to stand in front of Lisa again.

"How did you do that?"

"I gather from Sandy that Fraser proposed to you the night he arrived back from Holland, the night I drove him home. Is that right?"

"Yes, it is."

"Well, on the way down I told him about Miss Roy's death and that you owned Breck House, and I suggested that the time was ready for him to make an offer for it."

"What did he say?"

"Only that he had already thought of that. Did he make an offer?"

"Yes, he did. I had to refuse to sell because of the conditions of the will. He wasn't pleased," said Lisa hesitantly, recalling the unpleasant expression on Fraser's face when she had told him about Aunt Maud's will.

"And soon after that he asked you to marry him?" persisted Sarah, her eyes glinting with devilry.

Lisa did not reply at once. She was thinking of that moonlit night when the scent of lilac had been heavy. Had Fraser proposed marriage to her or had she suggested it to him? She found she wasn't sure any more.

"Yes, I believe he did," she replied vaguely.

"Then there you are," said Sarah, flinging her arms out wide in a dramatic gesture. "It's as clear as day. He wasn't thinking of Johnnie at all. He was thinking that if you were his wife you could hardly refuse to give him permission to build on your land, especially after you'd been married to him for a while. He wants to marry you because he wants Breck House."

CHAPTER VIII

HALF an hour later Lisa sat at the kitchen table in Breck House and held her aching head on one hand while she wiped away salty tears with the other. She was still shaken and alarmed by the bout of weeping which had overtaken her as soon as she had reached the house. Not for years had she wept like that; like a tired, disappointed child.

But why the disappointment? Pushing lethargically to her feet, she went over to the sink, filled the kettle and plugged it in. She would make some tea, that cure for all upsets of the mind. She only wished she had someone to share a cup of tea with – Ina perhaps. But she would have to drink it alone. The price of independence, she thought with a grimace, was having to deal with problems alone.

As she reached into the cupboard to get out the tea caddy she answered her own question. She was disappointed because she was afraid Sarah's suggestion that Fraser wanted to marry her because he wanted Breck House was true. Thank heaven she had had the presence of mind not to betray her disappointment to Sarah, who probably would have revelled in it. Keeping her cool, she had said to the model in as steady a voice as she could muster,

"But of course I know that. You don't think I'm such an innocent to enter into such an arrangement with a man like Fraser blindly without knowing what he's about? It's his business and mine, not yours or Sandy's."

And then while Sarah was still staring at her wide-eyed and a little shocked she had added,

"Would you mind waiting for Fraser here? There are some things I must attend to at Breck House and I don't like leaving Johnnie alone in case he wakes up and is frightened. Fraser shouldn't be long. You might tell him too that his supper is on the oven keeping warm."

Then she had swept out of the house and had not stopped running until she had reached the friendly comforting darkness of the old house on the brae.

It hadn't been a bad performance, she thought, but she hoped Sarah had stayed until Fraser had arrived because she had a feeling he would not be pleased if he found Johnnie alone. However, for all she had been able to hide her hurt from Sarah she was still left with this awful suspicion that Sarah had been right, and that she had been blind when she had said she would marry him, having forgotten the occasion of their first meeting when he had said he would do anything to get his own way. That laconic "anything" had included marrying her.

What should she do? Confront him with the suspicion and see how he reacted?

The kettle boiled and she poured boiling water into the tea-pot, pretending that it was the steam which was causing globules of moisture to form on her cheeks and not tears.

"Lisa!" Fraser's voice was sharp and she almost dropped the kettle. She put it down carefully and spun round to look at him. He stood in the entrance to the kitchen from the hall. His eyes and hair were very dark against the unusual paleness of his face and she had the impression he was very angry about something.

"How did you get in?" she stammered foolishly.

"How do you think? Through the front door. I knocked twice and when you didn't answer I tried the handle and found the door was unlocked. Were you deliberately ignoring my knocks?"

"No ... no. I didn't hear them, or the door bell." How foolishly she was behaving, like a child caught in the act of doing something she shouldn't.

He was coming across the room towards her. He would see the tears on her cheeks, and he could not bear women who wept.

"Would you like a cup of tea?" she asked desperately, turning to the cupboard where the crockery was kept.

160

"Yes, please, I would," he said, and to her relief he sat down at the table. "I came to thank you for cleaning up the house. I'm afraid it was in a bit of a mess."

"Why didn't you tell me Mrs. Wilson wasn't cleaning for you? I'd have come and tidied up."

"I never thought of asking you," he replied easily. "After all, we aren't married yet."

"Oh, so you'll expect me to clean up as a matter of course when we're married?" she retorted, feeling a strange lift to her spirits, as she reacted automatically to his teasing, and he grinned appreciatively although his eyes narrowed observantly as she moved towards the table and he was able to see her face clearly.

"It will be entirely up to you whether you clean it or not," he returned, and then with concern deepening his voice he asked, "What did Sarah say to you?"

"Then she did wait for you? I was hoping she would, because I didn't want to leave Johnnie ... Oh, have you left him alone? Will he be all right, I mean...."

"He won't come to any harm for an hour while you tell me what went on between you and Sarah. It must have been unpleasant if it's made you cry."

"Me?" she exclaimed jauntily. "Oh, I never cry."

"No? Then why is your face all blotchy and why are your eyelashes spiky? It can't be some new form of make-up," he said dryly.

"It isn't blotchy," she protested, and went to peer in the mirror above the sink. "Oh, yes, it is," she muttered, looking quickly away from her reflected face. She picked up the teapot, crossed to the table and began to pour into one of the cups.

Clear hot water came out of the spout!

"Red Smith, you are in a bad way," he mocked gently. "Sit down and I'll make the tea."

Lisa collapsed into the nearest chair, put her elbows on the table and clasped her head in her hands. Behind her she could hear the kettle boiling again, the tea caddy being opened and closed, the water being poured into the pot and then the click of the pot's lid as it was put in place.

Fraser came back to his chair and put the tea-pot on its stand.

"It will be infused in a few minutes. I can't stand unbrewed tea. Please note for future reference," he said.

"There won't be any future for us," she replied, looking at him. He raised an eyebrow at her as he slid down in his chair, hands in his trouser pockets, and stretched his legs under the table. His hair was ruffled and dark stubble blurred his chin. The colour had returned to his face and he no longer looked angry. He looked more like a man who had worked hard all day, had enjoyed his work and was now ready for some relaxation ... and some fun. Judging by the gleam in his eyes the fun was going to be at her expense.

"Because of what Sarah said to you?" he prodded.

"Yes."

"Are you going to tell me what she said or am I going to have to shake it out of you?"

She was a little alarmed. He had never touched her once in all their strange association, and the thought that he might take hold of her now and shake her now made her feel dithery. She was not sure how she might react.

"She said that you want to marry me because you want Breck House," she replied hurriedly. "Is that true?"

"To a certain extent, yes, it is true. The thought had crossed my mind some time ago," he said smoothly. "Does it make any difference to you?"

"Of course it makes a difference! You deceived me. You didn't tell me that was why you wanted to marry me," she said furiously.

"I have many reasons for wanting to marry you and I haven't told you all of them ... yet. I just dangled in front of you the one which I thought would interest you at the moment ... and you bit," he explained coolly.

He picked up the tea-pot and poured tea. The fluid flowed

in a golden-brown stream into a cup. Disconcerted by his answers, Lisa stared at the big hands performing the homely rite of pouring tea and adding milk, so efficiently. They were strong hands. Were they also loving hands capable of taming a wild heart?

He pushed a cup and saucer in front of her together with the sugar bowl and asked if she had any biscuits.

"I enjoyed my supper," he said, "but there just wasn't enough of it."

When she had found what he wanted Lisa sat down again and began to sip her tea.

"So Sarah came to cause trouble, did she?" Fraser observed. "She must have been annoyed about something."

"She was. About you and me getting married. She said she'd been to see Sandy and he was very upset . . ."

"I thought he might be," he put in quietly. "In fact it was his interest in you that pushed me into taking action sooner than I might have done."

"That and Aunt Maud's death," she suggested acidly.

"Another contributing factor," he drawled, and over the top of the cup which he had raised to his mouth, his eyes glimmered with amusement. "Did it never occur to you that I might marry you for your property?"

"No. Because I know very well that it remains my property by law no matter whom I marry, and you can't make me give you permission to extend the boatyard on to my land."

He was smiling to himself as he poured more tea into his cup, that faintly wicked triumphant smile.

"That's very true," he agreed. "Then why are you all steamed up about Sarah's suggestion?"

Lisa became very interested in the tea-leaves at the bottom of her cup. The reason for her being steamed up, as he called her behaviour, had just flashed through her mind and she did not want to admit it as yet, least of all to him.

"I don't like being deceived," she said rather weakly.

"Is that all?" He sounded very sceptical.

"It may be funny to you, but to me it's important."

"And because I haven't told you everything about myself you want to back out?" he asked.

"Yes, I do. I don't think I can go through with it," she replied in a choked voice, still peering into her cup as if she could find solace there.

"So just because a jealous woman vented her spite on you you would let Johnnie down," he accused quietly.

The cup clattered as Lisa placed it hastily in the saucer.

"Oh, you ... you ... devil!" she exclaimed. "You know I can't do that to him."

"I hoped you couldn't, because I would have had a hell of a time explaining to him," he admitted. "Can I assume then that we can go ahead as planned?"

"Yes," she muttered, not looking at him.

"You know, I suppose, that Sarah was also wild because she discovered that Sandy Lewis had fallen out of love with her and that she blames you?"

"He isn't in love with me. He only thinks he is," she answered.

"Tell that to Sarah. One of the reasons why I proposed marriage to you was that I hoped to divert your attention to me so that he would get over his infatuation with you and remember she was around. But she seems to think it's too late. That's why she ripped into you tonight," he said.

"Oh, and that was one reason why I agreed to marry you, too," she admitted. "I thought that when Sarah realised you weren't available she would turn to Sandy and ..." Her voice faltered to a stop as she realised what she had just done. She had admitted to having an ulterior motive for marrying him too.

"Nothing to choose between us, is there, Red?" he jibed, rising to his feet. "It's time I went home. I'll pick you up tomorrow early in the morning to drive into Kilbride and get this business with the registrar fixed. Don't bother to come to the door. I saw myself in, so I can see myself out," he added, turning to her as she moved to his side.

His unexpected turn brought them very close together and Lisa stepped back defensively.

"Perhaps it's time I sealed our bargain too," he said. There was a mischievous twinkle in his eyes and she retreated again, being brought up short by the table. She did not want him to kiss her because she was afraid that they both might find out too much about her real feelings concerning him.

"Don't make me hate you, Fraser," she warned him, hoping to deter him.

But he was not deterred. He stepped after her, reached out a hand, grabbed the edges of her knitted cardigan near the throat and pulled her forward.

"That's a risk I'll have to take," he replied with a laugh, and kissed her firmly on the mouth. She was just thinking that there was nothing shy and feather-like about this possessive kiss when fireworks seemed to explode in a shower of sparks behind her closed eyelids and immediately all her resistance collapsed. But she had no chance to respond because he moved away, and before she had opened her eyes he was in the hall and calling out,

" 'Night, Red. Sleep well. See you in the morning."

Surprisingly enough she did sleep well, better than she had for nights, and she was ready and waiting when he came to pick her up to drive into Kilbride. They took Johnnie with them to save him going on the school bus, so there was little opportunity for conversation between her and Fraser on the way there. As they came out of the office Fraser saw an acquaintance of his waiting by the bus stop who wanted to catch the ferry from Ardmont to Gourock, so they gave him a lift. When they dropped the man at the pierhead Lisa got out of the car too because she wanted to go to the mill. With a wave of his hand Fraser drove off to the boatyard, and judging by the faraway expression on his face his mind was already taken up with the day's work ahead of him and Lisa Smith was the last person he thought of.

At the mill Lisa found the atmosphere extremely uncomfortable. Sandy was sad and vague, and Ina was silent and reproachful. Anyone would think she had committed a crime in consenting to marry Fraser for convenience, thought Lisa impatiently as she walked home. If the two of them had gone around holding each other's hands and gazing into each other's eyes, swearing undying love for each other, everyone would have been delighted and there would have been messages of congratulations from all sides. As it was only her father seemed pleased. From Sandy she had received reluctant good wishes, from Ina reproaches, and from Sara spite.

She had to admit to feeling a little guilty about Sarah and Sandy. She felt she must make amends somehow. Eventually she decided to go to see Sarah, having first phoned to make sure that the model was at home.

She was greeted over the phone by Bunty Chisholm, who promptly invited her to lunch, saying that she wanted to see Lisa about a suit she would like her to design.

Lisa accepted the invitation and an hour later set off in Aunt Maud's old car. Driving along the road, high above the twinkling water, she recalled the last time she had come that way and the car had boiled on the hill. Today was quite different. Spring was in the air. The sun was shining and visibility was good. She could see right down the northern arm of the strait to the distant hills of Ayrshire.

Stopping the car in the lay-by where Fraser had found her that wet winter's day, she got out to stand and stare for a moment. Far below her the narrow stretch of fertile land which bordered the strait was being ploughed by a bright red tractor. Beyond the freshly-turned earth the water was translucent green changing through amethyst to deep, deep indigo and then to black in the shadow cast by the tall conifers which grew on Eilean Glasa, the Grey Isle.

On such a day her spirits should be sky high and although they had a tendency to float that way when she remembered Fraser's kiss of two nights ago she kept having to subdue them telling herself that it had meant nothing to him. He had merely been indulging his sense of humour, making fun of the way Sandy had sealed a bargain. It had not been a loving, tender embrace even though she had had an inclination to respond to it.

When she reached the castle there was no sign of Sarah and for the first half hour she spent a pleasant time with Mrs. Chisholm being shown various parts of the castle. When eventually they returned to the long lounge which looked out over lawns which swept down to the River Creddon, Sarah was there, slim and lovely in a plain green dress, lounging in an armchair, sipping sherry. She shot a sulky glance in Lisa's direction while Mrs. Chisholm poured sherry for herself and her guest.

"What are you doing here?" she demanded.

"Lisa has come to see you, dear," said Bunty sweetly. "Although I thought I'd take the opportunity to have a little chat with her myself. Well, here's to you and Fraser, Lisa. I'm so very pleased for you both and so is Harry." She raised her glass in Lisa's direction and then sipped a little of her drink. "We'll have lunch in the morning room and then I'll leave you two together, because I have to go into Inverey. It's my turn of duty at the hospital."

All through lunch Bunty kept up a flow of conversation about her voluntary hospital work so that the awkwardness between Lisa and Sarah was not noticeable, but when she had gone Sarah made no attempt to hide her hostility.

"If you've come to ask me to model more clothing for you, you can forget it. I don't want to have anything to do with you, or with Fraser . . . or with Sandy Lewis," she added.

"That isn't why I've come," replied Lisa, suddenly seeing Sarah for what she was – a very spoilt child. "Although I think it's very foolish of you to take that attitude towards Sandy, who hasn't done you any harm ever, in spite of the way you treated him years ago. I've come to explain that I didn't deliberately set out to make him fall in love with me, as you seem to think, and to tell you that he isn't in love with me anyway."

"But he was so upset about you and Fraser. He kept on

saying he couldn't believe you were like that."

"He was upset because he had found out that I was different from what he'd expected. He'd built up an image of me as his soul-mate, his partner for life who could do no wrong and who would rush to do his bidding and transform his life for him. He has some very old-fashioned ideas about women. He treats them as if they're something precious, yet expects them to be subservient at the same time. That's a tall order."

Some of Sarah's sulkiness vanished and she looked at Lisa with interest.

"I suppose you're right, and that's what I found so restful about him when I came back in December, met him on the boat and found him just the same, very courteous and a little shy. But he didn't show any signs of still being in love with me and I was piqued," she said slowly. "So I tried to attract his attention in the only way I know how, using the one available man ... Fraser ... whom I found attractive too. It didn't work."

"No, it didn't work with either of them, did it? You can't bear a man to ignore you, can you, Sarah?" commented Lisa.

"No, I can't." Sarah jumped to her feet and began to stride up and down the room. "Oh, what a fool I am! Peter warned me. Peter's always warning me, has been for years. He warned me about Jack. I should take more notice of him because he's nearly always right. He knows me so well. You get to know a person very well, you know, when you're with her every day, for hours, taking her photograph."

Before she realised what was happening Lisa was listening to Sarah's confidences about Peter Wright, about the awful things he did and said to her, the way he pushed her around.

"Mother would have a fit if she knew," finished Sarah with a sudden giggle.

"But you really like him to behave like that, don't you?" said Lisa. "You'd rather have that than no attention at all."

Sarah looked surprised.

"Yes, I suppose I do like it. It's better than that casual,

please-yourself attitude that Fraser has to a woman. How do you put up with it?"

"I must be going," said Lisa evasively, not wishing to admit that it was his casual attitude which made her prefer Fraser to Sandy.

"Oh, must you go? Just when we were beginning to understand each other," complained Sarah petulantly. "That's what I've missed in my life, having a girl-friend to talk to. I'm sorry I was bitchy to you the other night, but everything seemed to pile up inside me. You seemed to have had all the luck with the only two eligible men in Ardmont without so much as lifting an eyebrow, without trying even, and I had to get at you somehow. Forget what I said earlier about not wanting to model the tweeds. Any time you like."

"Only if Peter Wright is the photographer. You wouldn't look quite the same if he wasn't there to push you around and be rude to you."

Again Sarah looked surprised. Then she giggled as understanding dawned on her.

"Do you know, Lisa, I think you're right. Thanks for coming."

Vaguely pleased at the outcome of her interview with Sarah, Lisa wondered what to do about Sandy. If he was going to behave as he had after Sarah had let him down eight years ago he was going to ruin his life. She sensed his discomfort at her presence in the mill and knew that she would have to take drastic action soon. She could not work under such conditions any more than she had been able to work for Richard Hatton.

One morning Sandy's melancholy and his meek deferential treatment of her got on her nerves so much that she turned on him and said crisply, "It's no use, Sandy, I can't be a partner. It's . . . it's like being a prisoner. I can feel my creative urges dying for want of air. I'm stifled. I shall have to break the contract."

"But what about the designing you were going to do?" he

169

complained anxiously. "You can't let me down like this."

"I'm not going to let you down," she replied desperately, wondering how she could make him understand. "But I will if I'm tied. Can't you see I have to be free to design properly? Once I feel that I have to design because you're dependent on me I can't do it. Let me freelance and I'll never let you down."

He stared at her consideringly.

"Och, very well," he muttered resignedly. "I suppose I was a fool to think that I could ever tame you. But I'm beginning to think Fraser is going to have his work cut out keeping you in order."

"I shouldn't waste time worrying about him," she retorted tartly. "He's more than equal to the task. But there's something I have to tell you and I'm going to tell you here no matter who is listening in. There is someone in this village right under your nose who would make an excellent partner in your company, far better than I would be because she's practical and level-headed. She'd also make that partner for life you're looking for. But because you're her employer and the manager of the mill, she thinks you're completely out of her reach. Being the warm-hearted person she is she'll be contented to adore you from a distance while remaining your faithful employee. Think of all that love going to waste, Sandy, while you sit here yearning for the unattainable. There, that's all I can say, except to apologise for not living up to your expectations. But I'm only human, not a goddess to be worshipped or a slave to run to your bidding."

While she was speaking his face had gone red and then white as he'd reacted to her words, but the melancholy had gone.

"Don't apologise," he said gruffly. "I'm human too and just as much to blame. I realise that. You see, I was so afraid of Sarah when she came back that I turned to you. I should have known better. I wonder if you're right about Ina."

"Well, there's only one way to find out. Surely you know

the truth of the saying about faint hearts by now, Sandy Lewis," Lisa retorted as her parting shot.

It gave her a great feeling of satisfaction to play at being fairy godmother. She had done her best to make amends to both Sandy and Sarah and she was sure that now she had pointed out to them that Ina and Peter were their natural partners they would both take some action in the right direction instead of yearning after someone totally unsuitable.

CHAPTER IX

TIME was passing in a blur of April showers and calm sunny periods. Buds were swelling and birds were nesting. A gradual change was taking place as the new growth of grass began to assert itself in field and garden. Blackthorn bushes were a-blaze with tiny white flowers and hawthorn hedges were showing bright green tufts as leaves burst out of the fine spiky branches.

Another change was also taking place as more yachts were launched and took up their positions at their moorings. They brought movement and colour to Ardmont Bay as they swung slowly round every time the tide ebbed or flowed. Winter with its wild storm and moments of frosty brilliance was over and soon the village would be full of summer visitors.

The boatyard buzzed with activity. Most afternoons Lisa met Johnnie as he came home from school, gave him his supper and put him to bed, because Fraser was so busy. The only time she saw him was when he returned to the white house for his supper after Johnnie had gone to bed, and then she left him with hurried instructions about his meal and went back to Breck House to sew the suit she was making to wear on the first of May.

Not once did Fraser make any effort to detain her, to talk to her about the day's events or to ask her what she had been doing. His usual reply to her excuse for leaving was an absent-minded nod of agreement before he disappeared upstairs to wash off the grime of the day.

At first Lisa did not mind such casual treatment, being only too glad to make her escape. It was all part of the arrangement between them, she reminded herself, that neither should make any unnecessary demands upon the other. Fraser had a deadline to meet where his work was concerned and she could understand him being absorbed in that work because she behaved like that herself when she was working on a design.

Still, it would have been pleasant if he had invited her to stay with him while he ate his supper or had shown appreciation occasionally of what she was doing for him.

He never did, and the first of May loomed up with nothing more said about the arrangements for their marriage. And although Lisa knew that the announcement was still in the window of the registrar's office and that both Sandy and Ina had been asked by Fraser to be witnesses, she began to wonder if Fraser himself had forgotten that he was to be married.

The thought occurred to her as she watched him on the last day of April supervising the launching of Harry Chisholm's big schooner, which had now been re-named *Sea Saga*, the fifth of Harry's boats to be given that name. She felt a sudden freezing of her heart and acknowledged ruefully that she would be unable to bear it if Fraser had forgotten.

The big black boat slipped into the water, creating a miniature tidal wave which swept up over the shore and on to the road. Fraser turned with a triumphant grin and shouted to her,

"That's the last. Now we can get married!"

Suddenly embarrassed by Wally Scott's grin and the amused cracks made by some of the other men, Lisa turned and walked away into the yard where Fraser caught up with her.

"Don't tell me you'd forgotten," he jeered.

"No. But I thought perhaps you had," she retorted.

"And that worried you?" he was quick to ask.

Her step did not falter and she kept looking straight ahead, refusing to rise to his baiting.

"Not really," she lied coolly. "If that's the last boat to be launched this week I suppose you won't be working late this evening, so perhaps you'll be able to put Johnnie to bed. He'll be pleased if you do, because he hasn't seen much of you this week."

"Fair enough," he said, equally cool and casual.

"What time shall I see you tomorrow?" she asked.

"Ten o'clock at the registrar's. I want to be back in Ardmont to catch the eleven-thirty boat for Gourock. I'm taking Wally and young Weir with me to sail the boat back. You bring Ina with you tomorrow and I'll take Sandy."

Was ever a marriage arranged so casually? thought Lisa, as she walked up the brae to Breck House. Perhaps she ought to call it off now because to continue might bring heartbreak for herself. Her hands clenched at her sides. This was the nearest she had come to admitting that the impossible had happened and that she, of all people, had fallen in love with a man who was quite obviously not in love with her.

Next morning was fine and clear. The sun was there behind a film of grey haze which covered the sky. Later it would break through and the day would be warm. Lisa dressed in the new suit. It was a soft shade of blue and had a long straight skirt which had a slit in it to allow for freedom when walking. The jacket was waisted and had wide lapels and under it she wore a blouse of frothy white lace. On her head she placed a wide-brimmed hat, and as she picked up her matching white gloves and handbag she realised she hadn't any flowers. Tears pricked her eyes suddenly. It was her wedding day and no one had thought to provide her with any.

Ina arrived in good time and together they drove through the village and out on to the moor road which wound inland to Kilbride. Half an hour later they walked into the registrar's office where Fraser, looking remarkably spruce in a finely-checked tweed suit, was waiting with Sandy. As Lisa walked in he came to meet her and presented her with a small posy of violets.

Unable to look at him because emotion at the sight of the dark velvety petals of the shy delicate flowers threatened to overcome her, she asked,

"Where did you find them?"

"Under the hedge in my garden," he replied. "I'm afraid I forgot to order any others, so I was up with the lark seeing what I could find. They're a little early, due to the mild weather we're having."

Touched by the gesture, Lisa could only thrust her gloves

and bag at Ina to hold while she pinned the posy to the lapel of her jacket with a brooch she was wearing, and then followed Fraser into the room where the brief ceremony was to take place.

Within an hour they were back in Ardmont walking along the pier towards the yellow-funnelled steamer which was ready to leave. Ina and Sandy had left them and had gone to the mill and Lisa had only a thick gold band on her finger and a posy of violets pinned to her jacket to remind her that she was married.

"You don't know what a relief it is to know that Johnnie will be with you," said Fraser. "It will make all the difference to going away. He wanted to stay off school and come with us to the registrar's office, but I wouldn't let him. I said that it was something strictly between you and me."

"Did he object?"

"Of course he did. He seems to have a fixed idea that you are entirely his property and his alone. You'd better start putting him right about that before it starts causing trouble."

"Why would it cause trouble, and with whom?" Lisa asked with an air of innocent surprise.

He grinned down at her as the boat's siren wailed to warn passengers not yet aboard that it was about to depart.

"That's something for you to puzzle about while I'm away," he said. "I should be back Thursday night some time if this weather holds, just in time for Harry's schooner party."

"Schooner party? What's that?" asked Lisa, finding it difficult to hurry in her long skirt.

"We're invited to go with the Chisholms with about seventy other people on a cruise up Loch Creddon so that he can introduce his latest and biggest boat, not only to all his friends and relations and business contacts, but also to all the other boats he's owned. It's a crazy childish idea and only Harry could get away with it. Didn't I tell you?" he shouted to her as he stepped aboard.

The gangplank was pulled back, the embarkation gate was closed and the steamer began to sidle away from the pier.

"You never tell me anything!" yelled Lisa across the intervening strip of water and saw him laugh as he turned to talk to the two men from the yard who were going with him to fetch the boat from Ireland.

That night Lisa slept at the white house in the spare room next to Johnnie's. There had been a few slightly confusing and embarrassing moments when Johnnie had insisted that she move into his father's bedroom straight away. In answer to her calm statement that she preferred the spare room he trotted out his usual argument.

"Jim's mummy sleeps in his daddy's room. Jimmy says all mummies sleep with daddies."

"Yes, I know," Lisa answered. "But you see this is slightly different. Your daddy isn't here and I think I'd better wait until he comes home."

To her relief Johnnie seemed satisfied with this answer and helped, or rather hindered her, in the process of making up the spare bed, but she began to wonder after a while how much of the conversation would be relayed to Jim, thence to Jim's mother and thence round the whole village.

The spare bed was not very comfortable, having lost most of its springiness and having developed a hollow in the middle out of which Lisa had to climb in the morning. She decided after the first night that as soon as Fraser returned she would have her bed from Breck House moved into the room. She was quite sure there was not the slightest chance of her being invited to share Fraser's room as she had suggested to Johnnie.

She did not have much time in which to ponder on the strangeness of her situation because the day after Fraser left she met Bunty Chisholm and was soon involved in the preparations for the schooner party.

Bunty, neatly dressed in navy blue trousers and anorak and wearing short yachting boots, was crossing the boatyard when Lisa met her. When she asked for Fraser and was told that he'd gone to Ireland she looked astonished.

"But you were only married yesterday," she exclaimed. "Why aren't you on your honeymoon?"

Completely nonplussed by this question, Lisa found herself blushing and muttering about Fraser having to fetch a boat from Ireland immediately, or lose a client, and about it being difficult to go away on a honeymoon because of Johnnie.

"Well, I could mind Johnnie for you. There's nothing I'd like better," said Bunty. "I'm very fond of children. I only wish Sarah would settle down and present me with a grandchild. She's gone to London to see Peter – she wants him to come to the party. She seems very attached to him, but Harry and I find him a little strange. What do you think, Lisa? I'd hate her to make another mistake."

"I think Peter understands Sarah," replied Lisa cautiously.

"Well, I suppose that's a step in the right direction. I'm just going out to the yacht to see that everything is all shipshape for Saturday. I'd be glad if you'd come with me. You might be able to make some suggestions."

And so Lisa set foot upon a sailing yacht for the first time in her life. Fascinated, she stood and looked up at the two masts, the foremost one slightly shorter than the thick solid main one. Glinting gold in the sunlight, they soared up against the blue of the sky.

Then she went below down the neat stairway and was amazed at how much space there was. The original stowage holds had been converted into a comfortable living accommodation. There was a huge saloon furnished with comfortable settees and an extending table. It had fitted cupboards and bookcases and there were even framed pictures on the panelled walls. Further exploration revealed a big galley with every modern convenience for cooking, several small bedrooms with comfortable bunks, a toilet and a wash room complete with shower. Looking round admiringly, Lisa now understood why the carpenters at the yard had been working overtime.

"We're very pleased with the conversion," said Bunty as they returned to the big saloon. "Fraser has done a good job. Now when we arrive at the anchorage at the top of Loch Creddon on Saturday I think we'll serve a buffet luncheon. There'll be about six other yachts beside this one, including *Madrigal*. Harry wants to serve champagne only as it's a sort of celebration of his forty years of sailing, and I thought we'd start with smoked salmon and follow that by various cold meats and salad, with fruit and nuts to follow. What do you think, dear?"

Helping Bunty plan the party took up all of Lisa's spare time that day and the following day, and Thursday arrived without her realising it. It was a fresh blustery day with a strong southerly wind blowing up the kyle; a wind which would blow Fraser back home.

The thought excited her and she found herself looking forward to his return, but by ten o'clock at night when the wind had died down and the kyle was calm once more there was no sign of the yacht he was bringing.

Lying wakeful in the narrow humpy bed, Lisa hoped nothing had happened to delay his return, and she was just beginning to doze off when she heard the front door which she had left unlocked purposely open and close. The sound was followed by the thud of rubber sea-boots being dropped in the hallway and immediately she tensed and her heart began to beat faster. There were more noises from below, the sound of the kitchen light being switched on and off followed by the switching on of the landing light. The stairs creaked as Fraser walked slowly up them and she heard the soft pad of his feet on the bare wooden floor of the landing. The handle of the door to his bedroom rattled as he turned it and then there was a profound silence after he had opened the door.

Then to her surprise she heard the sound of his feet coming across the landing towards her open door. Against the yellow oblong of light his form was a dark silhouette as he stood there looking in. Lisa found she was incapable of sound or movement. He stood there for about a minute, then moved away. A few seconds later she heard his bedroom door close and she let out the breath which she did not know she had been holding and let unexpected disappointment have its way with her.

The next day Fraser was up and out in the yard before she

178

arrived downstairs, but he came back to have breakfast with Johnnie. He was just the same, Lisa thought, saying very little about the trip across the sea from Ireland, answering Johnnie's questions absently and, judging by the lack of questions on his part, having very little interest in what she might have been doing. When Johnnie had left to catch the school bus, he went upstairs to shave, and it was when he came down to the kitchen again that she asked him about moving the bed from Breck House.

"Please yourself," he replied maddeningly. "It's your bed."

"Thank you very much," replied Lisa, thoroughly irritated by his disinterest. "But I'll need help to move it. Do you think ..."

He looked at her then and the coldness of his expression repelled her slightly. What had happened to the man who had given her a posy of violets which he had picked for her from his garden?

"If you want one of the men to help you shift it you'll have to wait until next week," he said curtly. "They'll all be too busy today."

He went out of the room and soon she heard the crash of the front door as he slammed it behind him.

For a moment Lisa stood biting hard into her lower lip, telling herself that it had been silly to indulge in hopes and longings while waiting for his return last night. She must always remember that she was there for Johnnie's sake and that she must not make any unnecessary demands on Johnnie's father.

The day took its course. She went once more with Bunty Chisholm to the schooner to make sure all the preparations for the party had been made. She took the dogs for a walk, met Johnnie and made supper. Fraser was no more sociable at the mealtime than he had been at breakfast time and only spoke to her to tell her when they would be leaving to go aboard *Sea Saga* in the morning and give instructions on the sort of clothing she and Johnnie would require. Then after he had seen Johnnie to bed he went back to his office saying that he had some drawings of a new yacht he wanted to finish so that he could show them to one of Harry's friends who would be present at the party. After looking out the necessary clothing and sitting for a while on her own watching the T.V. in a desultory fashion Lisa went miserably to bed, wondering what she had done to offend Fraser so soon in their married life.

When she looked out of the bedroom window next morning she was glad to see that the water was calm. A slight mist hung over it and was still there, clinging to her hair and sprinkling Fraser's hair with glittering drops of moisture as he rowed her and Johnnie out to the schooner in a dinghy.

On board she waited for the arrival of Bunty and Harry while Fraser rowed back ashore to bring Willy Scott, the foreman, and his wife aboard. Within half an hour there were about twenty people on board, including an elderly man called Skip Burnett, who had taught Harry how to sail. With the Chisholms Sarah and Peter arrived bringing with them a tall fair young man whom Sarah introduced as her cousin Brian Sutcliffe.

"Look after him, Lisa, will you?" said Sarah. "He's from your part of the world and he sometimes feels lost amongst these clannish Scots."

Soon *Sea Saga*'s decks were thronged with guests. The men were mostly interested in the rigging and the marine equipment on board and the women spent their time admiring and exclaiming over the more domestic details such as the size of the galley, the comfort of the saloon and the convenience of the shower in the bathroom.

The mist thinned and as it cleared the sun came through. A light breeze blew from the south.

"Perfect, perfect," crowed Harry. "Just what we need. We'll hoist every sail and run up Loch Creddon in style."

Most of the men aboard being sailors of boats themselves, there were many willing hands and soon all sails were set. The mooring was cast off and *Sea Saga* slipped gracefully through the water, a big black bird with white wings, passing Ranald

Gow's big yawl which cast off its mooring almost immediately and followed the schooner up the kyle.

But by the time they had reached the islands at the narrows the pleasant breeze had died away and as *Sea Saga*'s bow pointed to the entrance of Loch Creddon the engine had to be started. Ahead lay five other boats, all of them becalmed, and as the schooner approached Lisa could see that three of them were called *Sea Saga II, III, IV.*

"I rowed the first *Sea Saga*, all fourteen feet of her, out into Loch Creddon this morning, and anchored her," Brian told Lisa as he leaned beside her on the bulwarks and watched the pine-clad slopes of the north shore of the loch slide by.

Having discovered she came from Manchester too he had stuck to her like a winkle to a rock. It wasn't a case of looking after him as trying to lose him for a few minutes, thought Lisa. And to make matters worse Johnnie, resenting Brian's attempt to monopolise her attention, had behaved badly several times, so badly, in fact, that he had already drawn Fraser's ire and had received a sharp set-down. At the same time Fraser had given her a reproving glance, obviously blaming her for his son's bad manners. Not that he had much time for noticing what either of them were doing. He was too busy talking to old acquaintances, giving advice to Harry on the handling of the schooner and sharing jokes with Sarah.

By the time they reached the head of the loch it was past noon. The weather had turned warm and muggy, and Brian commented that he wouldn't be surprised if there was a thunderstorm.

All the *Sea Sagas* were tied up alongside each other with the most recent acquisition in the middle, its two masts towering above the others. The other boats anchored nearby and soon everyone who had been invited was swarming on to the schooner to help themselves to the champagne and the food which had been set out in the saloon.

After having collected some food for herself and Johnnie Lisa took the boy up to the bow of the schooner. For once they had lost Brian and she hoped that Fraser might join them. But he did not appear. And why should he? thought Lisa disconsolately. Last time she had seen him he had been having a perfectly enjoyable time with Sarah.

Suddenly without appetite, Lisa set her plate on one side and leaned against the bulwark, steeped in misery, only vaguely aware of the laughter and gaiety of the people around her. Below her the water looked dark and turgid, having none of the colourful clarity it possessed on a clear sunny day. Above, ragged grey clouds circled menacingly and on the shore the trees, through which she could just glimpse Creddon Hall, soughed suddenly as a wind from nowhere whipped through them.

Johnnie had found a piece of rope and was pretending to fish. He had climbed on the bulwark and was balanced precariously on his knees leaning over to look down into the water. Lisa was just about to warn him to be careful and to grab the back of his jersey when the very thing she was trying to prevent happened. He fell overboard into the water.

"Daddy!" he shrieked, then his mouth was promptly filled with water and he sank.

Lisa's only thought was that Fraser would hate her if she let his child drown. Kicking off her shoes, she clambered on to the bulwark and dived into the water just as a clap of thunder resounded round the hills.

Water came up over her head in a smooth green wave and the shock of its terrible icy cold penetrated her clothing. She surfaced quickly and looked around for Johnnie. Rain was falling, hitting the water with big drops, and thunder rolled ominously again. Lisa saw Johnnie dog-paddling madly and she struck out in his direction. She thought she could hear voices calling to her, but the sizzling sound made by the raindrops as they hit the water faster and faster in a deluge made it difficult for her to hear properly. The sodden weight of her wet clothing was pulling her legs down so that she could not kick effectively. Spitting water out of her mouth, she looked round to see if she was anywhere near Johnnie. Something hit her on the side of the head and she lost consciousness.

CHAPTER X

THERE was a pain in her chest and every time she took a breath the inside of her windpipe felt as if it had been rubbed raw. Knives seemed to be sticking into her stomach and it heaved suddenly with nausea.

A familiar voice said,

"She's coming round now."

She opened her eyes and looked straight at Fraser. He was kneeling beside her, bending over her. Behind him she could see the trees moving in the wind. Rain dripped on her face and thunder rumbled distantly. She realised that she was lying on the ground and that she was wrapped in a thick blanket, with another blanket lying over her. Turning her head, she found Sarah on her other side, also kneeling and looking at her with anxious blue eyes. Her honey-coloured hair was soaking wet and hung in damp tails around her delicately-moulded face.

A pain throbbed on the side of her head and memory came back with a rush. Trying to sit up, she demanded hoarsely,

"Where's Johnnie?"

Fraser pushed her back.

"Take it easy," he ordered sternly. "Johnnie's fine. Brian and Bunty have taken him to the castle."

"What hit me?" she asked, raising a hand and feeling the bump on the side of her head.

"A lifebelt which some idiot threw to you. You sank, but fortunately came up again. Sarah and I were able to grab you and bring you ashore and apply artificial respiration while Brian and Bunty rescued Johnnie. As soon as Brian comes back with a car we'll take you to the castle and put you to bed," Fraser said brusquely. His face was pale and dour, and his crisp hair had been flattened by the rain.

"Mother will look after you," said Sarah comfortingly.

"You're very wet," Lisa murmured.

"Not as wet as you, dear," grinned Sarah. "The heavens just opened after you went over the side. Poor Daddy, I'm afraid his party is spoiled. Here comes Brian, I think. Will you be able to walk to the car, Lisa?"

"I'll carry her," said Fraser. "Thanks for your help, Sarah."

"Don't mention it. I was glad to help. It wouldn't have done for you to have lost her after only being married for a few days. I'll go back to the schooner now and tell everyone you're all right and try to cheer up poor Daddy."

She rose to her feet and walked away. Raising her head, Lisa watched her push off a dinghy which was pulled up on the small beach at the head of the loch, step into it, sit down and begin to row.

"I'm too heavy for you to carry," she said weakly to Fraser.

"Be quiet and do as I tell you," he ordered, and she had to bite her lip to control an urge to burst into tears. She had very nearly drowned and he showed not the slightest bit of emotion.

Following his terse instructions, she stood up with his help. Her head swam and she was glad of his support. Wrapping the two blankets round her, he heaved her into his arms and started to walk towards the car which was just stopping at the end of a rough road a few yards away.

"Never do that again, Lisa," he burst out suddenly.

"But I was afraid that Johnnie would drown," she quavered.

"You nearly drowned," he retorted in a tight voice. "Never jump into the water to rescue anyone until you're sure there's no other form of rescue available. Today there were plenty of dinghies and plenty of people capable of manning them and rescuing Johnnie. There was no need for you to fling yourself after him fully clothed. The water was quite calm and he's able to keep himself afloat in such conditions. Didn't it occur to you that I'd taught him how to take care of himself if he ever fell overboard?"

He was angry. She could feel the anger throbbing through him; see it in his white face and darkened eyes – angry because she had tried to rescue his child. If she had not felt so weak she would have slid from his arms, told him he was an ungrateful beast and made her way to the car on foot. But all she could do was turn her face against his chest so that he would not see her tears, and mutter into his damp sweater,

"I did it for you."

Two hours later Lisa was in bed, wearing one of Sarah's nightgowns, in one of the guest rooms at Creddon Hall. She had been examined by Dr. Clarke, who had been called in by Fraser to make sure that she and Johnnie had escaped serious injury, and then she had been ordered to go to sleep and had been left alone. Since she had an overwhelming desire to sleep she turned on her side and slept almost immediately.

When she awakened the sky outside the narrow latticed windows was dark. No noise from other parts of the castle penetrated the thick door of the room and for all she knew she could have been quite alone in the building. The feeling of having been deserted persisted, giving her a sense of panic.

Where was Fraser? Where had he gone when he had left her after telling her to go to sleep? Was he in the castle or had he returned to the schooner? Moving cautiously, she eased herself up in bed and stretched out a hand to her right. After groping for a while she found the switch on the bedside lamp. Rose-coloured light filtered through the big parchment shade, dispersing the gloom and restoring her spirits a little. Lisa leaned back against the pillows and looked round. The room was circular and she guessed it was in one of the turrets. Its predominant colour was rose pink and the furniture seemed to be made mostly of rosewood which gleamed warmly in the soft light.

In a mirror above the dressing table opposite the bed she could see herself reflected. A pale wedge of a face topped by spiky red hair; eyes wide and dark; shoulders surprisingly creamy where they appeared out of the scooped neckline of the nightdress. She looked vulnerable, a little lost, not at all the independent, self-contained person she tried to be.

Irritated by the image, she threw back the bedclothes. She

would get up and assert her independence. She was just about to swing her legs out of bed when the knob of the door turned. Startled, she pulled the clothes up around her and watched the door open and Fraser appear.

He must have been back to Ardmont, because he was dressed in a tweed sports jacket, dark trousers and was wearing a shirt and tie. He walked across to the bedside and stood looking down at her.

"Have a good sleep?" he asked.

"Yes, thank you. I was thinking of getting up."

"Don't bother. Stay where you are. Doc Clarke said you wouldn't feel back to strength until tomorrow or even the day after. Are you hungry?"

She nodded. If he had married her for love he would not be so matter-of-fact, she thought rebelliously. He would have taken her in his arms, kissed her and told her how glad he was that she had not drowned. Instead he stood, hands on his hips, his eyes dark and unreadable, his mouth a straight line, giving nothing away.

"Bunty thought you might be, so she's having a tray prepared for you. I'll go and get it," he said.

As he went towards the door she experienced again the panicky feeling at the thought of being alone again. It was so unusual that she sat up, clutching the bedclothes about her.

"How is Johnnie?" she asked, in an attempt to detain him.

"Fine. He's fast asleep in the room above this," he replied, and went out of the room, closing the door.

She was alone, frighteningly alone. She could only assume that it was shock which had produced the feeling and she determined to deal with it. She would get up, put on the long pink quilted dressing gown she could see lying conveniently on a chair, and sit at the small writing table which was set beneath the window. Lying in bed she felt too weak, incapable of coping with the man who was her husband. However, when she stood up eventually she felt remarkably dizzy and had to sit down on the edge of the bed quickly. Her head had hardly stopped swimming when the door opened again and Fraser came in carrying a laden tray.

"Where do you think you're going?" he asked as he placed the tray on the bedside table and turned to survey her.

"I thought I'd eat sitting at that table over there," she said, very conscious of his interested glance at her bare legs and feet which showed below the hem of the short nightdress.

"And you couldn't make it," he observed dryly. "Well, back you go. This tray has legs on it and will fit across your legs and act as a table, so you'll be quite comfortable. I'll fix the pillow for you."

As he reached behind her to plump up the pillows and set them against the headboard she protested,

"I'm not an invalid!"

"For the time being you are," he replied firmly.

Soon she was settled comfortably with the tray in front of her and was eating the thick broth which Bunty had sent with fresh rolls and butter. Satisfied that she was going to eat, Fraser walked over to the window and looked out.

"What time is it?" asked Lisa.

"About eight-thirty."

"Is the party over?"

"Yes, it ended with the thunderstorm. Harry decided to take the schooner back to Ardmont, I came back here with him because Bunty asked me to stay the night so I could be near you and Johnnie."

He pulled the rose-patterned curtains across the window and immediately the room took on an intimate atmosphere. Lisa leaned back with a sigh, having finished the meal, and he came across to remove the tray and put it on the bedside table again.

"You look better now," he commented. "Not so big-eyed and frightened."

To her surprise he sat down on the side of the bed quite close to her. As always his nearness tormented her and she looked away to the other side of the bedroom. On the curved wall there were some small pictures and she peered at them trying to make out whether they were original paintings or reproductions.

"Those are very pretty pictures, but I don't think they merit being stared at so intently," murmured Fraser mockingly. "What's the matter?"

"Nothing."

"Don't lie."

"Do I have to share my inmost thoughts with you as well as a bed tonight?" she asked querulously.

"You don't have to share anything with me, least of all a bed," he retorted acidly. "You made your thoughts on that aspect of marriage to me quite obvious when you decided to move into the spare room in my house. Don't worry, I can sleep with Johnnie tonight. He's in a bed three times too big for him."

The harshness of his reply startled her and made her look at him. He was not looking at her. He seemed more interested in the pattern of roses on the Chinese carpet. There was a bitter curve to his mouth and he was frowning. Lisa recalled the way he had hesitated on the threshold of the spare room the night he had returned from Ireland and realised suddenly that he had been as disappointed as she had been that night.

Realisation broke the bonds she had imposed on her love. She wanted to reach out and stroke away the frown and the bitter curve and to tell him he did not have to sleep with Johnnie.

"I know it's a pretty carpet, but I'm sure it doesn't merit being stared at so intently," she ventured, a quiver of amusement in her voice.

His head jerked round as if pulled by a puppeteer's string. His eyes were wide with surprise, but when he saw she was smiling he smiled too.

"You're right. It doesn't," he replied. "I much prefer to look at you. I've always liked looking at you."

Struck with a sudden uncharacteristic shyness, Lisa had difficulty in returning his gaze.

"So I'd noticed," she answered as lightly as she could.

"In fact that's one of the reasons I married you. I thought it would be pleasant to have you around to look at."

"Then why didn't you tell me?" she asked shakily.

"I thought it was a reason which wouldn't appeal to you," he replied provocatively.

"Where there any other reasons for marrying me which might not appeal to me?" she asked.

To her consternation he stood up. He was going to leave her alone again.

"Yes, but I'm not sure whether this is the time to tell you. You've had a harrowing experience and should rest. I'll take the tray downstairs."

As he stretched out his hands to pick up the tray she reached up and caught the nearest one. It felt strong and warm, a hand you could cling to when you needed comfort. But he didn't like clinging women who wept, she thought as tears welled in her eyes.

"Please tell me, Fraser," she whispered.

His hand closed round hers as he looked down at her.

"I need much more encouragement than that. You see, I have that abominable pride to settle with," he replied.

That pride behind which she realised now he hid all his hurts and disappointments. She stared up at him wondering what she could say or do, and all she could think of saying was the truth which was uppermost in her mind because her own pride had ceased to be a barrier.

"Please don't go away and leave me here alone. I know you don't like women who cling and weep, but I don't think I can spend tonight by myself after all. Please stay, Fraser. There's no one else in the whole world I'd rather be with than you."

He sat down on the side of the bed again, released her hand and grasped her roughly by the shoulders.

"Do you mean that?" he demanded. "And if you do are you prepared to take the consequences of what you've just said?"

Smiling through her tears, she reached up and put her arms round his neck and placed her damp cheek against his.

"I mean it. And I'll be glad to take the consequences. You see, I love you," she whispered.

Some time passed before she was able to speak again.

She asked, rather breathlessly, "Have you settled with your pride yet?"

She felt more than heard Fraser's familiar grunt of laughter as he held her close to him.

"I think so ... with your help," he murmured into the curve of her shoulder. "Thanks for saying it first."

"Saying what first?"

"That you love me. You see, one reason why I asked you to marry me was that I'd discovered I'd fallen in love with you, much against my will."

Amazed by his confession, she had to ask questions.

"Oh, when?"

"Is it important to know exactly when?" he laughed.

"Yes, because I'd no idea you loved me until now. You've been very secretive about it."

"I could say the same for you," he jeered softly. "I was attracted to you from the moment you set foot in my office, but I struggled against the feeling, partly because I distrusted it and partly because of pride. If you knew how many of my own words I'd been eating recently!"

"I've had the same problem," she laughed. "And I thought it was Sarah who was causing the strain. I thought you were in love with her and couldn't marry her because Johnnie didn't like her."

"It was your association with Sandy that had me bothered, and when I came back and saw you kissing on the doorstep I knew that I had to do something. I thought that if I could persuade you to marry me I'd be able to teach you to love me once we were living together. So I stooped pretty low in my own estimation and used Johnnie as bait."

Lisa was silent, thinking once again how easily she had risen to his bait. How well he knew her, far better than she knew him. But he had let himself be guided by love and now she

190

knew his was the loving hand to which she had tamed her wild heart.

"I think I began to understand your behaviour a little when you gave me the violets," she said, watching him walk across the room to the mirror to straighten his tie and subdue his hair. "But you were so cross and distant when you came back from Ireland that I began to have doubts again. I thought that you didn't want me after all, but just a mother for Johnnie."

"Not want you?" he exclaimed, turning to glare at her. "How do you think I felt when I found you sleeping in that old lumpy bed in the spare room?"

"Well, how was I supposed to know where I should sleep? You never told me," she retorted, glaring back at him. "Then you've been perfectly beastly today, flirting with Sarah and being angry with me for trying to rescue Johnnie."

"So I was flirting with Sarah was I? What about your behaviour with Brian? He scarcely left your side, he was so fascinated," he jibed. "Since you mention it, I was angry because you almost drowned before we'd had our honeymoon!"

"Oh, are we going to have a honeymoon?" she asked innocently.

He came across to the bedside table and picked up the tray and gave her an amused sidelong glance.

"Of course. I planned it before I went to Ireland. Beginning tomorrow, if you're better. I've borrowed a small sailing sloop from a friend and we're going cruising among the Western Isles. Didn't I tell you?"

"You never tell me anything," she complained to his retreating back as he walked to the door. "I know nothing about sailing."

"You'll learn fast enough," he said as he opened the door.

"But supposing there's a storm? Sarah said you don't like having a woman on board if there's a possibility of a gale."

He turned and looked at her, and her skin began to tingle.

"Depends on the woman," he replied laconically.

He was going, leaving her alone again, after all they had

just said and done. But it wouldn't do to cling because he might not come back if she did.

"Will you be coming back ... here ... tonight?" she asked, trying to sound casual.

"I'll always come back to you, Red," he said softly. "Remember that. See you later."

He went out and closed the door. Lisa leaned back against the pillows, her heart gladder than a singing bird's because at last it had been tamed by love.